For Charlie, Leo and Toby
Thank you for always being there

FLIGHT

Vanessa Harbour

Firefly

First published in 2018
by Firefly Press
25 Gabalfa Road, Llandaff North, Cardiff, CF14 2JJ
www.fireflypress.co.uk

A CIP catalogue record of this book is available
from the British Library.

ISBN 9781910080764
ebook ISBN 9781910080771

This book has been published with the support of
the Welsh Books Council.

Typeset by Elaine Sharples

Printed and bound by Pulsio

Chapter 1

If Jakob sneezed he could die. He pressed a sweaty hand over his nose. Every part of him was shaking. He could hear his heartbeat pounding in his ears as he peered out from his hiding place, tucked behind the straw bales up in the barn loft. Watching, waiting, praying.

'They say you're hiding a Jew boy,' the SS officer snapped. Jakob could see his pale face, his tight, thin lips. His eyes were hidden by a cap. Everything about him seemed brutal and sharp.

'What rubbish. Who told you that, Major Bauer? There's only me and my nephew here. He's no Jew boy, the authorities know that.' Herr Engel, Jakob's guardian, stared straight at the officer, not flinching, not giving any clue that everything he'd just said was a lie. He ignored the soldiers around him, stabbing their bayonets into the piles of straw and hay. But Jakob felt every thrust as if it was going straight through his heart.

Major Bauer smirked. 'It's not my business to tell you who. Just rest assured they're trustworthy.'

'Really? Is anyone trustworthy anymore? Fear and hunger make people mad and selfish, Major.' Herr Engel waved his arm around. 'Look, the horses are starving and we're starving too. Why would I hide another mouth to feed? There's already me and my nephew.' He shook his head.

'Maybe it's not *another* mouth – where is your *nephew*?' Bauer looked round.

His guardian rubbed his white beard. 'He's out, checking fences for me and collecting firewood,' he lied again.

Bauer strode up and down, pushing at sacks with his boot. 'Never really seen at school or in the village, is he? Bit convenient he's not here either.' He stopped. 'Or maybe that's your plan? If he's not a Jew, then maybe he's old enough to join the army. Tell him he has a week to bring his papers to SS headquarters.'

'Excuse me, sir, I know you're new to the area and I don't want to speak out of turn, but we've been here three years and everyone knows I need him. It's just me and him. It's too much work as it is – look at all these stallions.' He swept his arm in a flourish again. 'There's no time for education. Anyway, you don't need to read to shovel dung.'

Jakob gulped. That was the biggest lie yet. Herr Engel was a stickler for education. Every day, ever since he'd found him, he forced him to do lessons. The former Spanish Riding School Rider had very high standards.

His guardian sighed. 'Nobody's queried it before, so why now?' He spat before continuing, 'He's only fourteen. But yes, I'll tell him.' He hesitated, putting his head to one side. 'I could get his papers now if you want?'

Jakob held his breath. He had no papers, well, none that wouldn't get him shot.

Bauer looked slightly flustered. 'No, I want to see the boy myself.' He wasn't used to people calling his bluff, obviously.

Jakob breathed out slowly, wrapping his arms round his folded legs, holding himself tight.

'Of course. I'll tell him when I see him.'

'Taking me for an idiot is a big mistake,' said Bauer.

Herr Engel shrugged.

This seemed to irritate Bauer even more. He

raised his gloved hand and slapped the groom hard across the face. 'Show me respect, you old fool!'

Herr Engel stumbled slightly, putting his hand to his cheek.

Jakob wished he could jump down and beat the officer to oblivion there and then. He had the strength, he thought. Every muscle in his body tensed as he watched his guardian recover.

A sneeze began to tickle him again. He knew he mustn't move. Any sound would kill the pair of them. He held his nose and leant away from his peephole. A cramp ripped through his leg. He rubbed his calf hard, trying to massage the ache away. While he was distracted by the pain, the suppressed sneeze got its own back.

'Attishoo!'

Jakob froze. Had anyone heard? He peered out to see Allegra, his favourite stallion, pawing at the ground. He neighed loudly.

'I heard something.' Bauer angrily brandished a Walther pistol, scanning the stalls in the barn. 'Make that horse shut up or I will.'

A soldier walked in, raising his arm in salute. 'There's nothing here, sir.'

'There must be. Search again,' Bauer snapped,

waving his pistol at Allegra. 'I heard someone sneeze. Search the stalls in here.'

Jakob knew this was trouble. The Lipizzaner stallion would let no one in but him or Herr Engel. Allegra was already snorting, flaring his nostrils in protest.

'But...' The soldier hesitated a moment too long and Bauer turned to point his pistol at him.

'No buts!'

Clearly shocked, the soldier walked back out into the yard, barking orders. Several soldiers came running in and began to throw straw and hay aside and rip open sacks of feed. As they searched, they threw any horses' tack they found on the floor and stamped on it. Jakob could see the despair on Herr Engel's face. All because of him.

Allegra was panicking. Jakob felt it deep in his stomach. A dull gnawing ache. Peering down, he saw the stallion pacing in his stall, his coat dark with sweat. Now and then he stopped to paw the ground, tossing his head back and calling. Half snort, half whinny. No other horse made that noise. He was calling to Jakob.

'Calm down, boy,' Jakob said to himself. Forgetting everything, he focused on Allegra.

'Breathe with me.' He took in several long breaths, blowing them out slowly.

Allegra stood still, his head held high, neck arched, ears twitching.

'That's it, that's right! Breathe with me.'

Bauer glanced from Allegra to the hayloft. He thumped the stall door. The stallion jumped back, squealing.

'Don't forget up there.' He waved the pistol upwards.

A wave of despair enveloped Jakob.

He watched a plump, sweating soldier begin to climb the ladder.

Despair turned to panic. It started to overwhelm Jakob; he could out-run the soldier but not Bauer's gun. He had no way out and he knew it. Sweat trickled down his back. The cramp in his leg was agonising. Wiping his nose with his shirtsleeve, he said another silent prayer.

Amazingly, it was answered. With a roar, a motorbike screamed into the courtyard. The soldier stopped halfway up the ladder, turning to see.

The stallions pranced in their makeshift stalls, whinnying, seeking reassurance.

Bauer walked out to the yard and spoke to the

man on the motorbike. Jakob heard him shout, 'In the lorry now! We're needed elsewhere.'

The soldier scuttled back down the ladder.

Bauer strutted into the barn and sneered at Herr Engel. 'I'll return and I will find him. You can't fool me, old man.' Pistol in hand, he punched Engel hard in the stomach. His guardian bent double, grabbing at his abdomen, struggling for breath.

The stallions, Raluca and Allegra, kicked at their stall doors. Bauer jumped and raised his hand to Allegra. The horse lunged for Bauer's arm, baring his teeth.

'Don't, Allegra!' Jakob whispered.

The major stared at the stallion with a look of pure hatred. 'Don't you dare! Stupid nags, you'll soon be food for some hungry refugees. All your prettiness won't protect you then.' He drew his gun up and aimed straight at Allegra.

The grey stallion stared at him, his eyes wild.

Jakob watched, mesmerised, as without a moment's hesitation, Bauer pulled the trigger. The shot rang out around the stable yard. Blood sprayed across the stall.

'No!' Herr Engel's shout covered Jakob's scream.

His beloved horse crumpled to the floor and Jakob's heart splintered into a thousand pieces inside his chest.

Raluca neighed loudly and reared in his stall, pawing at the door.

For the briefest of moments, Herr Engel's grief-stricken eyes flicked towards Jakob. He sat back on his haunches, his eyes filled with tears. 'What will the Führer say when he finds out you killed one of the Spanish Riding School stallions in cold blood?'

Bauer swivelled, pointing the gun at Engel's face, the barrel under his nose. He snorted. 'Is that what they are? He won't give a damn. Anyway, if you say anything it'll be you next!'

Giving a final Nazi salute, he turned and strode out into the yard. His barked orders echoed around the barn, drowned out only by the slamming of doors and revving of engines.

As the trucks rumbled away, Jakob flew down the ladder, not bothering with the rungs. He fell to the floor, cradling Allegra's head. He buried his face in the stallion's mane, breathing in deeply. The horse's earthy scent was tainted with the metallic smell of blood.

'Oh Allegra, what am I going to do without you? Always there, right from the beginning. Oh Allegra…' he sobbed.

Herr Engel limped into the stall and rested a hand on his back. 'I know, but you still need to take care of the others.' His voice was rough with emotion.

They stared after the disappearing convoy. Neither cared that the sky was blue or that the sun shone; the blue had the brittleness of winter and the sun for them held no warmth.

Jakob felt empty. Herr Engel was right though. Raluca was pacing and calling from his stall, a desperate and piercing whinny, an empty cry for his friend.

'What are we going to do? How are we going to bury him?'

Herr Engel looked at Jakob, his eyes full of sadness. 'There's nothing we can do. He's too big for you and me to move on our own.'

'What? Just leave him?'

'We've no choice until I can decide what to do.'

Herr Engel disappeared, only to return carrying a bunch of sacks. He handed some over. 'Rip them open. Put the sacking over him first and then we'll use straw to cover him. We can't hide the smell but hopefully the other stallions won't realise. You know how much horses hate death.' His guardian shook his head. 'It's all so wrong.'

Jakob focused on tearing the sacking. Lost in their emotions, they covered the majestic stallion silently. When they'd finished no one would have guessed that underneath the pile of straw was a dead horse.

They stood, almost in reverence, until Herr Engel shattered the silence. 'Bauer enjoyed killing Allegra too much for my liking. Given the chance, he won't stop there.' He looked at Jakob. 'Move Raluca to one of the other stalls across the yard then muck out the others. I'm going out.'

'Where are you going?' Jakob wasn't sure he wanted to be left on his own or if he could manage the stallion. He could see Raluca staring wildly in his stall, his eyes rolling.

'It's time. I'm going to see Erich. He knows people and can get a message to the Director without that Nazi scumbag having any idea what we're about to do.'

Jakob ripped a bit of straw into tiny pieces. 'What are we about to do?'

'We need to go to Sankt Martin. The Director mentioned it in the past. It's safer there.'

'Sankt Martin? Isn't that the other side of the mountains?'

'Yes.'

'But we haven't got a lorry big enough to take all the horses.'

His guardian laughed, a hollow empty sound. 'I'm not planning on taking any roads.'

Chapter 2

In the yard Herr Engel grabbed a pitchfork and threw it to Jakob. 'Clear the stall around Allegra. Get rid of the straw with the blood on and his muck.'

Had he no heart?

'I thought you'd want to be the one to do it.' His guardian hobbled away, pulling on his old jacket as he went. He hadn't got too far when he shouted back, 'Make sure you move Raluca first, and do the rest of the stalls in there by the time I'm back.'

Jakob sighed. He walked towards Raluca's stall. The stallion paced up and down. Every now and then the horse would stop, toss his head high and neigh loudly, calling to Allegra. Jakob's heart felt heavy. The stallion stood, ears pricked, listening for an answer that would never come. His whole body quivered, rippling with muscle.

Raluca was a strong and compact stallion, the colour of a full moon and only slightly dappled these days. Soon he would be milky white. He'd been almost black when they'd moved a group of stallions down here to the farm back in 1942, three years ago. It felt like a lifetime ago. The Director had wanted to get Jakob out of Vienna, along with some of the stallions, including Raluca and Allegra. There'd been too many near misses with the SS and the Gestapo. It was away from everyone including the stud at Piber. The Director saw it as a chance to get some yearlings and young stallions out of Piber before the Führer sent all the mares and breeding stock away. The Director told Herr Engel – who'd achieved the rank of Rider in the Spanish Riding School by then – to 'take a detour on his way to the farm and magic them all away and then to keep their heads down'. A perfect plan. They'd done exactly that, until Bauer had moved into the area, messing everything up.

The stallion whinnied again, dragging Jakob back to now.

'You poor lad, he'll never answer, you know?' He moved into the stall. The horse startled when his footsteps crunched on the straw. Jakob heard him take in a deep breath, absorbing the familiar scent. 'Raluca, it's me. You're safe.' He clicked his tongue, reassuring him.

The stallion began to relax as he moved towards a motionless Jakob, lowering his head and nickering sadly. The horse gently blew air onto Jakob's outstretched hand.

Gasping, Jakob saw there were small splatters of Allegra's blood all over Raluca's head. 'Wait here.' Quietly and quickly he got a bucket of warm water and a cloth. 'Oh Raluca!' Very gently he wiped all traces of Allegra off the stallion and dropped the cloth back in the bucket with a splosh. The stallion pushed his head against him.

Jakob rested his head against the horse's forehead and with his spare hand he scratched the stallion's neck. Underneath his mane the hair felt short and soft. 'What are we going to do?'

The tears started. He'd always laughed when people said they were broken-hearted but now he understood. His own heart was shattered.

The horse pushed his head against him, over and over again. Sharing his pain.

Jakob sighed. 'Come on, lad, we'll move you away from here – when you stop pushing me, that is.' He couldn't help but smile.

The stallion nickered and nudged at him one more time.

'You'll need to be brave now. We'll have to walk past Allegra.'

Very slowly he moved forward, leading the stallion, putting his body between the horse and Allegra. Jakob watched Raluca's nostrils flare. He knew the stallion could smell the dead horse. He needed to keep him walking, but Raluca was having none of it. He pushed against Jakob with his head, over and over again.

'What are you doing?' Jakob stepped backwards.

Raluca did it again.

'Oh Raluca, we need to get you out of here.'

The stallion tossed his head and snorted, snatching the lead rein out of Jakob's hand. Before he could grab it again, the horse stepped round him and walked over to Allegra. Lowering his head, he sniffed the straw and sacking.

Puzzled, Jakob stood back and watched.

The stallion carefully took hold of the corner of one sack with his teeth, pulling it off to reveal Allegra's head. Jakob held his breath. The birds singing in the distance seemed very loud. What was Raluca doing?

The horse moved closer, ears twitching. He gently placed his muzzle on Allegra's head, nickering softly.

Jakob gulped. Pulling his sweater over his hand, he wiped away the tears trickling down his cheek. 'Goodbye, Allegra,' he whispered.

Raluca looked up at Jakob, then moved back to Allegra, nuzzling the stallion once more. He nickered a final farewell before walking towards the boy, his head held low. Jakob took hold of his lead rein. Raluca snuffled his outstretched hand, blowing hot air across it.

'Now I understand. You had to say goodbye too, didn't you? Come on, let's take you to a new stable.' He eased the stallion out onto the cobbles.

Jakob moved Raluca into a stall in the opposite part of the yard, nearer the food store and well away from Allegra. He moved as many of the stallions as he could to the spare stalls on that side.

'Raluca, who's going to help me join the Riding School now? Allegra understood me. We grew up together. He used to be the best at helping me to hide from the Nazis, back in Vienna.'

Raluca nickered, almost as if he was answering him. Jakob kicked the straw around in the stall, spreading it out with his foot. 'I was going to show Herr Engel how good we were. You know how many exercises I'd been doing with him.'

The stallion pulled some hay out of a freshly hung net, munching away, while Jakob put a bucket of fresh water in the corner.

'I've got to start all over again.' His shoulders slumped. He'd lost his best friend. He felt so alone.

Patting the horse's rump, he briefly smiled to himself. It had been good when Herr Engel had called him his nephew though, even if he had only said so to protect him.

It was over an hour before his guardian returned. He said nothing of where he'd been or what he'd done. He went straight into the house, which formed the third side of the yard, only coming back out later, when Jakob had finished moving and mucking out all the horses and the yard was shrouded in darkness.

'Supper?'

Jakob walked into the kitchen and collapsed into a chair. The fire was alight in the range.

'That smells good.' Jakob realised he hadn't eaten since breakfast.

'Nothing exciting. Goulash again, but it'll fill you up.'

Jakob didn't care, he was starving. The hot

paprika smell tickled his nose. He picked up the bread roll Herr Engel had placed by his bowl.

'Did you find Erich?'

Herr Engel nodded. 'The message has gone. Now we wait.'

Stuffing a chunk of bread in his mouth, Jakob mumbled, 'Couldn't we just go?'

His guardian served up his goulash and sat down. 'We can't go until I know they can take us and that the Director's happy. We need to be ready, though, as soon as word comes.'

Jakob dunked another piece of bread in the stew, chasing meat and potatoes round as he let the bread soak up the sauce. Trying hard to keep the emotion out of his voice, he whispered, 'I hope they won't be long. Bauer wants my papers, doesn't he?'

Herr Engel nodded. 'Hmm. That man's trigger happy. I saw it in his eyes.'

Jakob flinched.

The rumbling sound of a truck engine coming into the yard interrupted their meal. Jakob shot out of his seat, a knot of panic strangling his stomach. He could feel the colour draining out of his face. 'Bauer?'

Herr Engel pushed him back into his seat, shaking his head. 'No, don't worry. It's my arrangements.' He walked over to the window and lifted the curtain to check. He nodded at someone, then moved over to the gramophone. Soon the dulcet tones of Strauss's *Vienna Waltz* rolled around the room. He turned it up as loud as it would go.

The music brought back images of the dancing horses in Vienna. 'What's going on?' Jakob asked Herr Engel, tipping his head to one side.

His guardian sat down. 'Eat!' he said, digging into his stew again.

Jakob pushed the food around, taking the odd mouthful. He could hear strange noises in the yard. He could bear it no more. Pushing his chair back, he moved towards the door. Herr Engel grabbed his arm.

'No!'

'Why not?'

'It's Herr Fichter.'

Jakob fell back into his chair. 'The butcher?'

Herr Engel nodded. After a few minutes, he whispered, 'It was the only way. I couldn't let him rot.'

Jakob ran to the sink and retched. His head hung over the porcelain bowl.

'I had to do it, for the sake of the other horses.' His guardian shifted his chair. 'We've got to face facts. We're in danger. And it's not just Bauer. As I was coming back along the road, I passed thirty or forty hungry refugees. One of our horses could make a meal for them.'

Jakob spun round, unable to bear it. 'NO! I won't let it happen. They can't eat them and I'm not going to let Bauer shoot them either. I won't, I WON'T!'

Anger was etched across Herr Engel's face, his grey eyes hard as flint. 'And you think I would? I've no intention of losing any more horses ... or grooms for that matter. I've got a plan.' He scraped his chair back and walked over to a cupboard. He pulled out an old double-barrelled shotgun and loaded it. 'We'll take it in turns to stay on guard in the stalls.' He handed the gun over to Jakob. 'You can go first. This old body needs its rest!'

The gun felt heavy and unfamiliar in Jakob's hands. He turned it over and over. He had no idea how to use it.

'Point at what you want to shoot and pull the

trigger. Not that difficult,' said Herr Engel. 'Maybe I should've taught you sooner.'

'Would've been more useful than English and geometry.'

His guardian raised one eyebrow.

Jakob had to look away. 'Sorry.' He pulled the gun up to his shoulder and swung round to face Herr Engel.

'Whoa, it's loaded, remember!' he shouted, pushing the barrel away.

Jakob dropped the gun like a burning ember. 'Sorry,' he stammered. He felt so stupid. He pulled his sleeves down over his hands, feeling a flush of embarrassment creep up his neck.

'Don't do that either! It could go off.' Herr Engel sighed, retrieving the shotgun. 'You need to show the gun respect.' He cocked it. 'Look, this is how you reload it and get it ready to shoot.' He handed it back to Jakob. 'Go on, you have a go. Let me see.'

He did as he was told. At first he felt all fingers and thumbs. He wasn't used to holding something so big and deadly and he was convinced he would kill Herr Engel at any moment. He loaded and unloaded it a couple of times, before looking up at his guardian.

'Good! Keep doing it until it feels natural...'

Eventually Engel handed him a thermos and a couple of blankets. 'Now I think it's time. There's some coffee in there to keep you warm.'

Jakob walked out into the yard and shivered. The temperature had plummeted. Spring definitely hadn't arrived yet. He glanced over to where Allegra had been. There was no sign of the horse at all. They hadn't heard Herr Fichter go. Gulping back bile again, he went over to Raluca's stall.

'Hello, lad, mind if I sleep with you tonight?' He scratched the stallion's withers and clicked his tongue. 'Your coat has got much lighter over the winter, you know? It's just like that moon up there.' He pushed at the stallion. 'Shove over.'

He took spare straw and made a bed in the corner, putting a blanket across it before he lay down. 'Ouch!' He sat back up, pulling out bits of straw that had poked into his back. 'This is going to be a long night,' he sighed.

Jakob poured himself some of the coffee and sipped it. He didn't really like the bitter taste, but it did warm him a bit as the hot liquid reached his stomach. Lying back down, he leant on his elbow and looked up at the sky through the stall door. A dim and distant memory flitted into his mind. The deep black velvet sky reminded him of his mother's dresses. A time before the Nazis had spirited away his parents. A time long ago, before Herr Engel had found him hiding behind Allegra.

Jakob wondered where his parents were now. Dead? He sighed. That was something else he tried not to think about too often. He shook his head vigorously, trying to empty it of those fears. He looked at the stallion. 'At least you don't care who I am.'

Raluca, as if sensing his pain, put his muzzle on his shoulder and, huffing gently down his neck, nuzzled into him. Jakob smiled and rested his cheek against the horse's head, breathing in his sweet smell. Raluca nudged him and whinnied softly.

He must have dozed off. There was a rustling in the feed store.

Damn, what was that? He knew it was too loud to be rats, and it wasn't a noise the stallions made. He tried to rub the sight back into his eyes. They took a while to adjust to the thick blackness. Impenetrable clouds had blotted out any moonlight now.

His hand crept through the straw until his fingers curled round the cold metal of the shotgun. Slowly and carefully, he drew it towards him. His heart was pounding hard against his chest, the beat thrashing in his ears.

As quietly as he could while lying on a pile of straw, he pulled himself up to standing. Raluca stood to one side, letting him pass. Edging forward, he felt his way, relying on memory and his outstretched hand, feeling each step on the cobbles with his foot. He mustn't startle whatever it was.

The clouds fractured and half a bloated, buttery moon lit the yard. Jakob heard someone take in a sharp breath. He gulped and moved towards the noise. It definitely came from the feed store. He pulled the gun up to his shoulder and pointed the long barrel forward, just as Herr Engel had shown him. It stretched out in front of him, shaking. He said his silent prayers again.

The door to the store creaked open.

Jakob held his breath and edged further forward, watching the door, waiting.

A shadow moved out. The moon seemed to get even brighter. Jakob found himself staring into huge dark eyes, fear spreading in them as they looked straight down the barrel of the gun. A flat cap pulled well down hid any hair. Clasped in the figure's hands were two potatoes. He was obviously hungry. Should he blame him? How could he shoot him for a couple of potatoes?

His hesitation was enough – the shadow took its chance and ran.

'Oi!' shouted Jakob. He swung the gun into the air and his finger twitched at the trigger. A loud bang rang around the yard, startling the horses and sending Jakob flying backwards into a pile of straw. His shoulder throbbed.

The thief screamed as he disappeared. It was high pitched. Was it a girl?

Herr Engel opened the kitchen door. The light flooded out. 'What's going on?' he shouted.

'A thief.'

'Did you get them?' he asked, easing his stiff joints down the steps.

'No, I don't think so. They were stealing potatoes. See?' He pointed at the dropped vegetables still rolling around on the floor. 'Herr Engel, they didn't look much older than me. They only took two potatoes, and I made them drop them.' A lump of guilt stuck in Jakob's stomach. This felt all wrong.

'Damn them! Frightened the life out of me and all over two potatoes. A thief's a thief, though. Your age, you say?'

'Yes. Dressed like a boy, but I am sure it was a girl.' He searched the darkness and wondered where she had gone. The look in her eyes was imprinted on his brain. 'She was terrified.'

Herr Engel shook his head and took the gun off Jakob. 'This world is full of madness. We'd better settle the horses again. Two gunshots in one day are enough to frighten anyone, let alone these highly strung beasts.'

Jakob looked round. The stallions were pacing around their stalls and snorting. 'Sorry,' he mumbled.

After an hour of talking to the horses and calming them back down, he was exhausted. Well into the night, Herr Engel put a hand on his shoulder.

'Get inside, you look frozen. Go in and I'll take over the watch.'

The thought of a warm, soft bed was irresistible. He smiled at Herr Engel. 'Are you sure?' He prayed he wouldn't change his mind.

'Yup, go on, get to bed.'

'Thank you.'

With relief, Jakob went into the house, leaving the groom on guard.

He flopped into his bed. However, when he closed his eyes, sleep eluded him. Instead he saw blood splattering from Allegra's majestic head and the girl's eyes full of fear. He could hear Bauer laughing manically, standing above them shouting, 'I'm going to get you, Jew boy!'

He rolled face down, letting the pillow swallow his sobs.

Chapter 3

'Come in here, Jakob. We need to talk,' shouted Herr Engel from the tackroom.

By the time he got there, his guardian was already sitting in the corner, puffing on a cigarette. He'd picked up a bridle and was pulling the thread out of a broken section. Jakob hovered at the door, not quite sure what to do. The rich smell of leather and Herr Engel's tobacco enveloped him.

His guardian didn't look up. Instead, he muttered out of the corner of his mouth, the cigarette wobbling as he spoke, 'Sit down, lad.' He nodded towards a stool. Jakob did as he was told. 'Glad to see you've started to clean the tack they stamped on yesterday.'

'Thank you. It was my fault they'd made the mess after all.'

Herr Engel ignored this. He picked up a needle and stitched away for a bit. Jakob watched him force the needle through the old leather, intrigued. It didn't matter how many times he'd seen him do this, he was still fascinated.

'Things are moving faster than I thought,' said Herr Engel. 'Erich has just brought a note from the Director. Our messages must have crossed. The Director's concerned about the way the war's going in Vienna, too, and wants all the stallions together.' He pushed the needle through the other way. He took a deep breath. 'I've decided not to hang on. We're leaving tonight. I've sent a letter back to say as much.'

Jakob looked at him, surprised. 'What?'

Herr Engel's cigarette glowed red and the room filled with smoke. Wisps of white drifted up towards the ceiling. 'He's taking the rest of his stallions across from Vienna to Sankt Martin. He wants us to meet him there.'

Jakob didn't know exactly where Sankt Martin was, other than over the mountains. 'Are we leading them?'

Herr Engel worked quickly and deftly, before hanging up the finished bridle next to the saddle with military precision. He poured himself a coffee from his flask.

'Yes.' He took a sip. 'We're going to ride one each and lead the others. We need to get a good start, just in case Bauer does come back. He'll be furious and might start a search.' He peered over the lip of his cup.

Jakob didn't want to think about how easily they could be caught. He picked up the brushes and started cleaning the grey hairs out of them, making a pile by his side.

Herr Engel stubbed his cigarette out on the bench. 'Last night with the thief has shaken me, and the way Bauer is, it's definitely time to move. With any luck we'll reach Sankt Martin in a few days. It's about a hundred and thirty kilometres. If we can travel thirty to forty kilometres a night we should get there in three to four nights, with a good wind, that is.'

Jakob gulped. He'd never ridden for that distance before. He dragged the curry comb across the brush, tugging out clumps of grey hair, before mumbling, 'Will the horses be able to cope?'

'They've no choice if they want to live. Horses are a lot tougher than you think.' Jakob could feel his guardian's eyes boring into him, before he took another long sip of coffee and moved away.

'Anyway, today we groom all the horses, get the tack ready and then leave when the sun sets. You'll need to pack.' Herr Engel threw him an old carpet bag. 'Use this.'

Jakob went to the house, climbing the stairs with a heavy heart. The spring sun was shining into his room. Motes of dust danced in its rays. He wasn't quite sure how he felt. Excited? Scared? He stood and looked about him. There was a bed and a chest of drawers, that's all. No hint of who he was.

Pushing the chest of drawers to one side, Jakob lifted the loose floorboard underneath it and pulled out a small package wrapped in one of his old shirts. He placed it on the bed and unwrapped it. Inside was his treasure.

There wasn't much: a tatty, well-thumbed book of classical dressage he'd found on a stable floor back in Vienna. He flicked through it briefly. He knew every bit of it off by heart, all the pictures and all the words.

Next was a small framed photo of his parents. He ran his thumb over their picture and tried to remember what they'd sounded and smelt like. He wrapped them up again carefully, smoothing down the shirt. 'You can go in here,' he said, as he placed the package at the bottom of the bag. 'Safe and sound.'

He grabbed the few clothes he had and stuffed them in too, then went back to Herr Engel.

Chapter 4

'I want you to ride Raluca. He's full of good sense. Trust him.' Herr Engel stood in the stable, late in the afternoon. Jakob listened as intently as he could. They'd spent all day grooming and feeding the horses, getting them ready. Now he was shattered. He tried to stifle a yawn. Engel raised an eyebrow but continued. He handed him some rope halters and lead reins. 'You will be leading Flavory, Maestro, Pluto, Largo and Jupiter.'

Jakob's mouth dropped open. 'All of them?'

'Yes. Do you see anyone else?' His guardian made a dramatic sweep of the stables with his arm.

'But…'

Herr Engel dismissed his concerns. 'You can do it. I'll take the rest. Now tack them all up.' He strode away. 'Oh, and make sure the reins aren't loose and that the stirrups aren't hanging down.' He turned back. 'Put the rope halters over the top. All right?'

He went into the stable and Jakob was left standing in the yard, turning the ropes over in his hand. Would he really be able to do it? The thought of trying to control all those horses with just these ropes, and while on the back of a horse, was daunting.

His guardian's voice broke the silence. 'Be quick and quiet about it.'

Walking into the stalls, Jakob hatched a plan. If he acted confident…

The stallions seemed to be waiting for him. 'Well, boys, this is it! We're going on a little trip!' It almost sounded confident, apart from the slight crack in his voice at the end. Some of the horses nickered back a welcome. Maybe it had worked.

'Maestro, you're first.' Picking up a saddle and bridle, he walked into the jet-black stallion's stall. Jakob placed the saddle on his back. 'You know you have a huge responsibility, being the only black Lipizzaner in the yard? Jet black equals Sunday's child, which means good luck, see?' He gave Maestro's neck a consolatory pat. Sighing, he gazed up at the mountains. 'And we're going to need all the luck in the world.'

As he tightened the girth, Jakob couldn't stop his hands shaking. Catching his thumb, he shouted, 'Ouch!' and stuck his thumb in his mouth. Maestro whinnied in sympathy. 'Sorry, boy, that was my fault.' He shook his head. 'Jakob, stop being stupid.'

Working as quickly and quietly as he could, he moved to the steel grey, Flavory, who shone like metal when he was groomed properly. Then he went onto Largo, a flea-bitten grey.

Jakob laughed as he approached him. 'I don't know, next to those other two, who are both so sleek and shiny, you look like a child has flicked you with a black paintbrush, or you've been bitten by loads of fleas, of course. That must be why the colour's called flea-bitten, mustn't it?' He knew he was waffling. The boy winked at Largo when he'd finished, and moved on to Jupiter. 'You, on the other hand, your dapples look like a starlit night, so beautiful.'

Jakob tacked them all up without injuring himself again and led them out to the yard one by one, where he tied them to the fence. Jupiter's rope kept slipping through his fingers. 'My hands are so clammy,' he moaned. He rubbed them hard against his jodhpurs, trying to dry them. But it was pretty useless.

The enormity of what they were about to do weighed heavily on him. The air was thick with tension and the horses picked up on it and danced around.

'Just Pluto and Raluca to go,' he reassured Herr Engel, as he passed his guardian and strode into Pluto's stall. The stallion was fed up of waiting and snatched at his shirt, catching a bit of skin with it. 'Now that really hurt,' Jakob said through gritted teeth. 'Don't be like that, not today of all days.' He scratched at the stallion's coat, flea-bitten grey like Largo's, but his tone was brown rather than black. The mix of white and brown made him look a bit pink. Jakob always thought it was a funny colour for a horse. He could be a tricky one and today it seemed was one of those days.

A clattering echoed around the yard. Jakob's heart missed a thousand beats and Pluto pranced around, his hoof landing on Jakob's foot.

'Ow! What was that?'

Herr Engel shouted back, 'Sorry, it was me, I tripped over a bucket.'

Jakob blew his cheeks out and said to the

fretting stallion. 'It's all right, lad. Let's get you ready to go.'

The stallion tried to nip him again.

'Watch it! That really isn't very nice, you know.' Pulling his shirt out of the stallion's mouth, he tried to slip the snaffle bit in there instead, but the horse clamped his mouth shut. Jakob sighed. 'Not now, Pluto, do come on.'

Pluto threw his head back and shook it.

They didn't have time to play games. He had an inspiration. 'I know what I'll get you.' He turned on his heels and walked out, returning with a small lump of precious sugar in his open hand. He placed it carefully next to the snaffle bit. 'What do you think?'

Pluto was too greedy to resist taking both sugar and bit into his mouth at once.

'Good boy!' Relieved, Jakob slipped the rest of the bridle on. With his clumsy fingers he tried to do up the bridle buckles, but Pluto continued to prance around the stall. The stallion was in a mood now.

'Will you please stand still?' His irritation sliced through the air.

Pluto stared at him, almost daring him to move.

Jakob looked away. He knew better than to play Pluto's game. He'd been there too many times before. He closed his eyes, just long enough for Pluto to get bored. The horse came up and snuffled at Jakob's hand. He didn't respond, making the stallion wait before rubbing his neck.

'Was I not paying you any attention? Well, if you stop messing about, I will! All right, let's get your saddle on.'

Pluto blew air out of his nostrils and dropped his head.

'I know, I know, you really want to play, but today's not the day.' He placed Pluto's saddle on and the stallion eventually allowed him to tighten his girth. Then he led him out to the front, tying him to the fence. 'Wait here, I'm going to get Raluca.'

The stallion almost nodded, before starting to gnaw on his rope.

'Don't do that either!' Jakob laughed.

Getting the horses ready when they were determined to play the fool was exhausting work, and he still had one more to go. Jakob ran his hand through his hair. He took Raluca's saddle and bridle and pushed into the stallion's stall.

'Come on Raluca, just you to go. I know it's late.'

The horse nickered softly, nuzzling at him. The stallion behaved perfectly as the boy slipped the snaffle bit in and did up his bridle with still trembling fingers.

'You seem almost white in this light. Could you have a word with your mate Pluto about how to behave, please? You know exactly what to do. You are so patient,' he chattered as he struggled to do up the girth.

Lastly he needed to put the halter on. He knew he'd hung it up on the side of the stall with the hay nets, so he reached out for it. But his hands found no ropes or halter. He looked. There was nothing there. Where was it? He couldn't see it anywhere. This was mad. Jakob knew he'd brought it in with him.

Raluca snorted.

Jakob turned.

The stallion had the halter hanging from his mouth and a twinkle in his eye.

'What the...? You're wicked!' All the tension melted away as he roared with laughter.

Taking the halter from the stallion, he placed it on the horse's head. Raluca pushed his muzzle into Jakob and snuffled at his hand.

'It will be all right, won't it?'

The stallion nickered.

'I wish I could be as confident as you.'

He led the stallion outside to join the others. The sun had started to set and there were hints of mauve on the horizon. Herr Engel had all his stallions lined up and waiting too.

During the day, Herr Engel had packed everything that they and the horses might need into saddlebags. He had strapped the bags and blankets to several of the horses. Now he was tying his rolled-up blanket and the shotgun to the stallion he was going to ride: Monte, a grey with powerful hindquarters and stubby little legs but a big heart.

'I never thought I'd see the day when Lipizzaners were loaded up like pack horses,' said Herr Engel, shaking his head.

Jakob nodded. The elegant animals did look very strange indeed. 'Will they be all right?' They were a wonderful collection of different shades of grey, from almost white to Maestro's jet black. They were getting quite agitated, all holding their heads high, with arched necks. Many were dancing on their toes. 'They know something is up.'

'Of course they do. But they're tough, don't worry. Now put this extra sweater on and tie this round your waist.' He handed him a sweater and a belt with a knife sheath on it.

Jakob pulled the knife out of the sheath. It was a double blade and seemed very sharp as it glinted in the setting sun.

'You may need to cut yourself free if the horses play up. Leading this many horses is never going to be easy and certainly not when they're on edge like this.'

It sounded terrifying. Jakob pulled on his sweater. 'Hopefully they'll calm down soon.'

Herr Engel fiddled with Monte's girth. 'Now, if you go first and lead them to the woods, I'll follow on and meet you there. We can take the bridle path to the river and then we can follow that. Sound reasonable?'

Jakob had no idea, but he had no alternative and it got them away from Bauer. He nodded.

'Up you get then.'

Jakob untied Raluca and jumped up on his back, slipping his feet into the stirrups.

'Have you got the knife?' Herr Engel double-checked.

Lifting his sweater, he showed his guardian. The stallion danced. Jakob swung him round to face Engel.

'Good. You're not going to be able to hold all five ropes and the reins in each hand, you need to tie some to the others. Let me show you.' He grabbed the ropes with his gnarled hands, which were trembling, Jakob noticed, and twisted them round one another, tying them together. Maybe he was worried too.

Herr Engel touched his hand briefly. 'You *will* be able to do it, you know.'

Before long all five horses were attached to Jakob. They snatched at their bits and pulled at the ropes.

'You ready?'

He nodded.

'Don't worry, they'll settle down soon. Now off you go.'

Jakob took a deep breath, squeezed his legs lightly against Raluca and clicked his tongue. The horse looked behind briefly before moving forward.

Allegra had been his favourite but Raluca had always ridden well too, luckily. The stallions behind didn't follow immediately. Only when the ropes tightened did they get the message. Plus Herr Engel slapped Pluto on the rump.

'Go on, boy!'

That woke him up. He jumped forward, dragging the others.

They trotted out of the yard. The hooves, clattering on the road, sounded like thunder to Jakob. It was only a short trip to the field, but it felt like an eternity. He kept looking around. Were the Germans waiting to swoop on them?

Herr Engel was right; the horses began to settle and not snatch at the ropes quite so much. 'Come on, boys,' he whispered, 'time to take you home.'

Chapter 5

Jakob tried to stretch the ache out of his arms and legs. Not easy with so many ropes and reins to keep hold of. He'd never ridden for this long before and his body was screaming. He dropped his feet out of the stirrups, allowing his legs to dangle down. The reins slipped through his hands and Raluca's head drooped.

'There you go, does that feel better?'

The stallions had settled and were following behind, only pulling occasionally. With his relatively free hand, Jakob tried to massage his forehead to ease his pounding head.

'What else?' he laughed to himself. 'Got to keep going though.' He shifted slightly in his saddle. If only he knew how long it was until the clearing. He was beginning to wish he'd looked at the map with Herr Engel. At least then he'd be able to visualise the distance.

'What did you say?' asked his guardian, turning briefly in his saddle.

'Oh, nothing.'

Around him still bare trees, with the slightest nubs of buds on their twigs, stood stark against the blackness. Branches grabbed at them as they passed. Jakob snatched his head away from their clutches.

Something moved in the corner of his eye. He stared into the woods. Was he imagining it? Questions and doubts going round and round made his head pound more. Who would want to follow them? Before he could say anything, Herr Engel slowed up and twisted in his saddle.

He whispered, 'We're coming up to the SS *Schloss*.'

Jakob felt like his head would explode. 'What?'

'We need to move as quickly and quietly as we can.'

Jakob looked at the twelve grey stallions. How exactly were they going to do that? 'They'll kill us,' he said. 'What if Bauer sees us?'

'We've no choice. We can't go by the roads.' Herr Engel's eyes were sad yet defiant.

Jakob felt sick to the pit of his stomach. Swallowing, he gripped the reins. Raluca tensed underneath him, his head coming up and his ears flicking to and fro. Jakob took a deep breath. 'Where is it?'

'We've got a bit to go. Round the next bend in the river, I think. But when we get there we should go by separately. Quieter that way. I'll go first then you move on my signal.'

Jakob strained to keep the stallions together.

Herr Engel whispered, 'You need to trust me.'

That was easy for him to say. Jakob glared at his stallions dancing around him, being anything but quiet.

'Oi, boys, stop pulling,' he whispered, gulping down the panic welling up inside him.

'They'll be fine. Stop worrying.'

'We could go back? I'm sure I could hide for a bit longer.' Jakob muttered, 'You said yourself the war won't go on forever.'

Herr Engel gave him a sharp stare. 'Don't be ridiculous, boy. It's not about you. Think of the horses.'

The stallions all shifted around, some pulling to snatch shoots of spring grass. Herr Engel was right, he couldn't risk them being shot. He sighed.

They moved through the wood until Herr Engel turned again.

'Right, we're here. Can you see the castle beyond the trees?'

Jakob peered through the gloom and could just make out a huge white building with long lines of windows on four floors. There were hexagonal turrets at each corner. It should have been beautiful, almost straight out of a fairytale, but he was too aware of what went on inside.

'Wait here until I give two flashes with my torch. Right?'

'All right,' said Jakob, sounding a lot more certain than he felt.

His heart slipped into his boots as Herr Engel and Monte walked off, followed by half the stallions, leaving Jakob waiting in the trees. Alone. Peering round, the wood suddenly seemed full of suspicious noises. Every crack and creak made him jump. Convinced the Germans were about to find them, his nerves transferred to the horses. Their ears were twitching, tails swishing. An owl hooted in the distance.

'Ssh,' said Jakob to no one in particular.

He watched closely for Herr Engel's signal, staring into the darkness. After what seemed like an eternity, the two flashes shone out. It was Jakob's turn.

He squeezed his legs and asked Raluca to move

along the bridle path. The stallion stepped forward easily, but the ropes round his wrists tightened, yanking him backwards and almost out of his saddle. The stallions behind weren't so willing.

'Ow!' He wanted to scream, but he sat firmly down in the saddle and pulled hard at the ropes. 'Get a move on!'

Finally they started to walk, dancing forward.

'Come on, boys!'

Hooves crunching on twigs and leaves sounded like drums announcing their arrival.

'Can't you walk quietly?'

Ahead in the darkness he could see swastika flags hanging from the windows of the *Schloss*, flapping in the wind. Close now, he held his breath and pushed Raluca forward, silent prayers running through his mind. Bile was rising in his throat, but he swallowed it down. He had to keep calm or the horses would panic.

They walked slowly along the bottom of the garden. In the moonlight he could see immaculate lawns were laid out in tiers above them, edged with large pots. Jakob had never seen a garden like it before. It seemed to go on forever. He just wanted to get away.

Their black-out windows weren't working; he could see shadows moving around inside. All they had to do was look out and they'd see him. His stomach crunched. This time he couldn't swallow the bile down, he spat the burning acid on the ground.

Looking up, he could vaguely see Herr Engel in the shadows. He must be about half way there.

The ropes tightened round his wrist and he gasped. He looked back. It was Pluto. Something had spooked him.

'It's all right, lad,' whispered Jakob as quietly as he could.

But the young horse wouldn't be calmed. Pluto's eyes rolled and his ears were flat. He half reared in panic. Jakob clicked his tongue, trying to soothe him ... and failing.

'Come on.' He couldn't help his voice sounding high pitched, etched with fear.

Pluto sensed it. The rose-grey stallion bucked and reared again. Jacob couldn't settle him. Sweat was pouring down Jakob's back. Pluto's terror infected the other stallions, who pulled too.

'I can't do this,' gulped Jakob.

He heard Herr Engel's loud, forced whisper. 'Cut the rope, set him free.'

Fumbling with the sheath, he pulled out the knife. The blade flashed in a moment of moonlight. Jakob looked up at the *Schloss* and all the air emptied out of his lungs.

There, a couple of metres away, at the top of one of the garden tiers, a soldier stood watching him. Not any soldier. It was Bauer!

Their eyes met.

But Bauer swayed. Jakob realised the officer could barely stand up straight. Tipping the contents of a brandy bottle down his throat before tumbling forward, Bauer shouted, 'Oh Pegasus! I shot one of those the other day. Maybe I'll shoot another!' He pulled out his gun.

'Cut Pluto free and run,' Herr Engel shouted. 'Now!'

But Jakob had frozen. He watched Bauer stumble towards him, brandishing the gun.

'Time to die, pretty horses…'

'Jakob, move!'

'Jakob?' slurred a halting Bauer. 'The elusive Jew boy?'

Pluto reared again, tugging on the rope,

dragging Jakob back to his senses. The SS officer was getting closer. He had to do something, fast, before he was pulled out of the saddle.

With two quick swipes, he cut through Pluto's rope. The stallion stared at him briefly before fleeing along the path, nostrils flaring and tail swishing.

Jakob knew he had to take a risk and move. Now. He pushed Raluca into a trot, pulling the remaining stallions with him. His arms screamed with the effort as he wrenched them forward.

Glancing back, he saw Bauer lurch down the garden shouting, 'Come back, pretty horses, I want to shoot you.' Waving his gun around, he tried to take aim. 'Stand still! I need you to stand still.'

'No! You're not shooting another one,' muttered Jakob.

As they rode past, Bauer held both arms up in an attempt to keep the gun steady. Instead he tripped over his own feet. In the corner of his eye, Jakob saw him tumbling down the bank. He heard shattering glass. Holding his breath, he glanced behind him, to see if the officer had got up. He hadn't.

Jakob didn't hang around. He urged the stallions seamlessly into a canter and on to Herr Engel.

'Keep going, don't stop,' shouted the groom, as Jakob and the stallions came towards him. He pushed his own horses into a canter too.

'That was Bauer. Knew it was me. Heard you call me Jakob.'

Herr Engel looked shocked. 'We must get away from here.'

Jakob could hardly breathe. 'Oh God … he fell … I don't think he got up … he was so drunk… What … about … Pluto?'

Herr Engel shook his head. 'We can't worry about him. He'll have to find his own way.'

Jakob started to say, 'I think…'

'Don't think, Jakob. Just ride. Come on.'

Jakob squeezed his legs against his stallion's sides, urging him to go faster. 'Let's get out of here, Raluca.'

Chapter 6

Jakob lolled in his saddle, his head drooping forward. Raluca shivered gently underneath him. He leant forward and hugged his neck.

'We'll get there soon.'

It was difficult to see beyond the trees surrounding them, but he could just make out mountains pushing skywards. The welcome sounds of the river as it rolled through the countryside echoed around him. Maybe that meant it wouldn't be too long until they got to the resting place.

In an effort to keep awake, Jakob searched around for any sign of Pluto. There was nothing.

'I'm sorry.'

'What for?' Herr Engel seemed surprised.

'Losing Pluto.' He knew how precious these horses were.

'If he's the only stallion we lose on this journey, I'll be more than happy,' said his guardian. He turned in his saddle and looked at Jakob properly. 'You're doing well, boy. Not many people can lead that many horses.'

Jakob nearly fell off his saddle. Herr Engel *never* complimented anyone. 'Are you all right?' he mumbled, scratching at Raluca's neck.

'Pardon?'

'Nothing.' Jakob smiled.

They fell into a companionable silence until they reached the river. Herr Engel twisted round once again.

'Let's stop for a moment, the horses need a drink. We've pushed them hard.'

'Are we nearly there yet?'

'Not quite.'

Jakob sighed as he dismounted. When he'd unravelled the ropes, his arms were red and raw. He tried to shake the stiffness out of them. Parched, he pulled a bottle off the saddle and took gulps of the lukewarm water.

'Eat,' said Herr Engel, handing Jakob a small chunk of bread and a bit of sausage.

He turned them over in his hands. He wondered what other food they would get on their journey. 'Thank you.'

'We'll eat more when we get to the resting place.'

The horses drank. Everything was the colour of night, shades of navy and grey.

Something made the hairs on the back of Jakob's neck stand on end. He started.

'What's the matter?' asked Herr Engel.

Jakob shook his head. 'Nothing, I'm seeing things.'

Herr Engel knelt down and filled his water bottle again. 'Now is not the time for nothings.'

'I keep thinking I see something. It feels like we're being watched.' He ran his hand through his hair. 'Could it be Bauer?'

Herr Engel laughed but his eyes didn't. 'I've never known a Nazi be quiet about anything and certainly not that SS scumbag.' Grabbing the boy's arm, he pulled himself up. He peered around, but Jakob knew there was nothing to see. 'Could it be people looking for food? Keep your eyes open.' He started to gather together his stallions' ropes. 'Come on, we need to go. Too dangerous to stand still for long, particularly if you're right.'

Jakob dragged his ropes together too. They'd been dangling in the water while the stallions had been drinking. Now they were sodden, making them much harder to manipulate.

'Go on, mount up, I'll hand them up to you.'

Jakob launched himself on to the back of Raluca. His muscles hurt so much he cried out.

'You've no stamina, boy,' Herr Engel laughed. He handed over the ropes. 'You will do by the end.'

Jakob wasn't so sure. He watched his guardian leap on the back of his stallion, taking all his ropes with him.

An owl hooted in the distance again. Jakob looked up. 'Do you think it's announcing our arrival to the animal world?' Swinging Raluca round, he said, 'You'd almost think there was no war going on.' But just as he spoke, the drone of Allied planes shattered the peace.

'Another raid on Vienna maybe,' said Herr Engel. 'Let's hope they leave the School alone.' His guardian grabbed his reins, turned and moved off.

Jakob followed, watching the outline of the planes high up in the sky. 'B-17s and B-24s.'

'What you say?'

'Nothing.' Knowing the name of Allied planes was a dangerous game. Planes were a secret passion of his. Not just his, it'd been his father's too.

The wind whipped around them, briefly shaking the trees, distracting Jakob from his plane spotting and making him look back down.

A flash of white streaked through the forest. There was no form to it.

'Did you see it that time?' asked Jakob.

'No. What?' Herr Engel swivelled round in his saddle.

'Something white over there.' Jakob pointed.

His guardian looked, but it had gone again. Away with the wind. A will-o'-the-wisp.

'Your imagination playing tricks?'

He shrugged. What could he say?

Where the ropes were wet they were really burning now. Letting Raluca's reins hang down, he rubbed at his hands and wrists. The stallion's head lowered as they plodded along. Thankfully the others had settled after their drink. They seemed to have learnt the rules now and Jakob was beginning to relax, almost enjoying the ride.

The trees began to thin and they came out into a clearing. There were green fields on both sides of the river leading to more trees in the distance.

Herr Engel twisted round. 'This is dangerous, there's a road up there.' He pointed to the left of the river. 'We need to move faster. We're really visible.' Gesturing ahead, he added, 'We need to head for those trees, can you see?'

The distant rumble of lorries on the wind broke the silence. It seemed to be getting closer. A brief look of panic swept across his guardian's face.

'Move now!'

Herr Engel didn't say anything more. He rode straight, into a canter. Jakob followed suit, Raluca moving effortlessly, all the horses spanning out. It must have looked like a white fan charging across the field. He kept Raluca heading forward. The wind flowed through his hair as the grass passed rapidly beneath them. The horses slipped into the woods, where they slowed to a trot, just as the first lorry rumbled round the corner.

Herr Engel wiped his forehead with a hankie.

'That was close,' said Jakob. He couldn't help but smile.

'Definitely. We need to keep going. I reckon another hour before we can stop.'

Chapter 7

Just over an hour later, Herr Engel led them into the clearing as a weak, milky sun peeked above the horizon. It was perfect, with lots of space for all the horses. They were surrounded by trees on three sides and the river on the other. Jakob checked and could see no houses or barns in the distance. He took a deep breath. The air was fresh and clean, mingled with hints of spruce and the damp forest floor. He felt good until he looked up.

In the distance the mountains stood guard. He sighed. They'd be the next challenge. He slid down from his saddle, stiff and sore.

'Let's get them settled first,' said Herr Engel.

Jakob undid the girth, slipped the saddle off Raluca, and placed it on the floor. He patted the horse, who was as sweaty as he was. Picking up a swathe of grass, he started to rub his coat.

'There, does that feel better? Let's get rid of that sweat and mud. I'll give you a good brush in a minute. You've done a good job tonight. Allegra would be proud of you.'

Jakob moved rhythmically across the stallion's coat, massaging the horse's tired muscles. 'What's the matter, lad? Can't you relax? You're breathing a bit fast too – are you in pain?' Examining him closely, he noticed Raluca was holding one front leg slightly awkwardly, resting his hoof on the grass. 'That doesn't look good.' He ran his hand gently down the leg. As he got near the knee, he found a large thorn sticking out of a lump. 'Damn!' He pulled the thorn out and threw it on the floor. He shouted across the clearing, 'Herr Engel!' before resting his hand back on the lump. It felt warm and Raluca flinched. 'I know, I know, I'm sorry.'

His guardian came over. 'What's the matter?'

'Raluca had a thorn in his front leg. Look, it's all swollen now.' He pointed out the soft swelling.

Herr Engel rested his hand on the leg too. 'Oh Raluca! Let's finish the others and then we'll get him sorted. Don't worry, though. I've got a cream.' He patted Jakob on the shoulder.

Reluctantly, Jakob left Raluca and he and his guardian quickly and quietly untacked all the other horses, rubbed them down and groomed them. When they'd finished, Herr Engel went over to the pile of saddlebags and started sifting through them.

Jakob watched, idly scratching at Raluca's withers. The horse snuffled at his head. 'What are you up to? Ah, I see, time for a bit of mutual grooming, eh?' Jakob laughed quietly. He put both arms round the stallion's neck, rubbing his ears, while the horse gently nibbled him. 'You may be poorly but you still look after me, don't you?'

Herr Engel was getting more and more agitated, throwing the bags and their contents around. 'For God's sake, where is it?' He emptied bag after bag. 'Have you seen my horse medicines?' he said, with despair in his eyes.

'No. I'll have a look too. They must be here.' Jakob quietly collected all the bits strewn across the clearing and replaced them in the bags. There was everything but the medicines. He shook his head.

His guardian sat down heavily on a log with his head in his hands. 'I must have forgotten it. I can't believe I didn't bring the most important bag.'

'So how are we going to treat him?' asked

Jakob. He didn't want to lose another horse. They had to do something.

'All we can do for him is bathe his leg with river water and pray.'

'It's got to be worth a try.' At that moment Jakob would have prayed to any god who would listen, if it meant saving his stallion. Taking hold of Raluca's head collar, he led him down to the river.

'All right, lad, in we go.' The two of them stepped gingerly into the water. It was cold and swirled around them, the current pulling at their legs. Jakob stood in front of Raluca, talking to him calmly, as Herr Engel worked at his side, gently bathing the swelling with the clear water. Jakob wasn't sure it would help as the swelling seemed to be getting bigger and bigger.

'You'll be OK, I promise.' He wished he truly believed that. 'I hope you can't read minds,' he mumbled as he scratched Raluca's forehead then leant his head against it.

The stallion blew gently into Jakob's hand, nickering quietly.

It wasn't long before Raluca was settled, resting with all the other horses who grazed on the sweet grass or drank from the river. His guardian had chosen a good spot, Jakob decided. He began to relax slightly. They could stay here quite safely during the day and no one would find them. He let out a deep sigh, as he rolled out his blanket, desperate for sleep.

Herr Engel stopped him. 'Let's set up a fire before we sleep. Go and collect some kindling. We need to eat.'

He glared at his guardian.

'Don't look at me like that. You'll be pleased when you wake up.'

Jakob trudged into the wood, stopping every now and then to pick up twigs and small branches. The dawn chorus echoed around him. The Nazis and the war seemed a hundred miles away.

A twig snapped in the distance. Jakob stopped, holding his breath. That didn't sound like an animal. He looked around to see if Herr Engel had followed him but he couldn't see anything. His heart was racing. Perhaps it was Bauer.

He shook his head. *Idiot! Stop panicking. It's a deer or something.* He carried on picking up wood. Every other moment, he looked up and round, listening hard for the slightest sound.

He heard something or someone pushing through the bushes, much closer this time. He blew air out of his cheeks, trying hard to pretend that he couldn't hear anything. 'I must have enough for a fire now. Time to get back.' His hands felt clammy as they grabbed onto the kindling. He spun round ready to go.

Jakob stopped in his tracks. The armful of sticks tumbled to the forest floor with a clatter.

There standing in front of him, half hidden in the shadows of the trees, was a horse. It was Pluto, with a girl sitting on his bare back.

'Thought you'd like your horse back,' she said.

He nodded. His heart was close to bursting through his ribcage, it was beating so fast.

'Can't you talk?'

Jakob stuttered, 'Are you alone?' He stretched his neck, peering beyond the stallion, searching for Bauer and all the grey and black uniforms.

'Of course,' said the girl.

'You've just appeared from nowhere with one of our horses, there's no "of course" about it.'

The girl shifted on Pluto's back. 'Well, that's not very friendly. I thought you'd be pleased I brought him back.' She leant forward and patted Pluto. 'After all, I did save him,' she smirked.

That stung Jakob. 'You've been watching us,' he

snapped. It all began to fall into place. The noises, the flash of white. It was this girl. 'Why?'

She looked down. 'I didn't want to be left behind.'

He stared into her face. 'It's you! You're the one who tried to steal the potatoes. I'll never forget those eyes.' Except this time they weren't scared, they were defiant.

'I'm sorry. I was so hungry.'

Jakob moved towards his horse. 'You must have been to steal just potatoes. Were you going to eat them raw?' He stroked Pluto, who nuzzled at him.

'No! I'd kill rabbits or catch fish to eat with them. I can look after myself.'

'This way.' He walked back towards the clearing, but she didn't follow. He turned around. 'Herr Engel will want his horse back.'

'But he won't want me,' said the girl.

'No, he won't, but...' He picked up the sticks and kindling he'd dropped.

'Look,' she murmured. 'I'm ... Roma.'

Jakob shrugged. 'Shows how little you know. He took me on and I'm a *Jew*,' he whispered, half to himself. He left her and walked back to the clearing. This time the girl followed with the stallion. He didn't look back but he could hear her. He smiled to himself.

Walking to the fire, he dumped the sticks and went to stand next to Herr Engel. 'We've got a visitor.' He watched the colour drain from his guardian's face.

'What the…?' Herr Engel grabbed the gun.

Pluto walked into the clearing with the girl sitting straight on his back. All the horses whinnied their welcome. Raluca slowly walked over and the two stallions rested their heads together, nickering.

'Pluto!' Engel snarled at the girl. 'Who are you and what do you think you're doing? You could've led the Germans straight to us.'

'I wouldn't do that,' she snapped back. Then she thought better of it and lowered her voice. 'I double-checked that no one was following me. I even went back on myself a few times to make sure. And I rode all over your tracks so no one could follow you.'

Herr Engel looked surprised. 'Hmm.' He moved over to Pluto and patted his neck. 'He looks all right. I thought we'd never see him again.'

'Don't worry, you don't need to thank me.'

Herr Engel ignored her. 'Where's his tack?'

'I took it off and threw it in the river. I can't ride with it.'

'Threw it in the river!' he shouted.

'I thought you'd rather I did that than the Germans find it.' She was rubbing Pluto's neck the whole time.

Jakob was impressed by her spirit. Now she was out in the clearing he could see her properly. She looked a bit shorter than him; her hair was dark and cut very short like a boy's. She was wearing boy's clothes which made her look younger than she was at first glance. She must be about his age, he thought.

Herr Engel noticed her makeshift bridle. 'You're Roma?' It sounded almost an accusation.

The girl nodded. 'So?' She held her head up high.

Jakob wondered if she was bracing herself for abuse because he saw her relax when Herr Engel put his gun down and said, 'Pull your weight and you can stay. Hungry?'

'Yes.' Her voice was a hoarse whisper, heavy with emotion. The eyes Jakob had stared into only a couple of nights before were full of tears.

'Get down and put him to rest with the others. Once you've done that, build the fire with Jakob.'

Herr Engel hadn't bothered with any pleasantries so Jakob tried. 'Do you have a name?' he asked.

'Kizzy.'

'I'm Jakob.' He pointed at his guardian. 'That's Herr Engel.'

'I know.' She dismounted and led Pluto down to the river.

Jakob was intrigued. 'How do you know?'

'I've been watching you for a while.' She turned to him. 'I saw Bauer murder your horse. The one you used to practise dancing with.'

Herr Engel raised an eyebrow.

Jakob looked away. He didn't want to remember.

'What's the matter with that horse?' Kizzy pointed at Raluca. 'He's lame.'

Jakob shook the image of Allegra's blood-splattered beautiful head out of his mind. 'He had a thorn in his leg.'

The girl knelt down by the stallion's knee. 'It's infected.'

'I know, but we forgot the medicine so we can't treat it.'

Kizzy gently stroked the horse's leg and Raluca nuzzled her head, his ears flicking to and fro. 'I can help. Wait here.' She hurried off into the woods.

'Why's she run off?' asked Herr Engel.

'She's going to help Raluca, apparently.' Jakob dragged his hand through his hair.

'You all right?'

Jakob shrugged, 'Yes, just tired.'

Kizzy came back into the clearing. 'I need to boil these up so I can make a poultice.' In her hand was a collection of what looked like weeds.

'What are those?'

'Only herbs, nothing dangerous, I promise. But they'll draw out the poison.'

Herr Engel looked closely, then nodded. 'Jakob, get some water.'

He did as he was told, then sat and watched as the girl boiled up the herbs before she ground them to a paste with a stone.

'I need something I can use as a bandage.'

'Use one of my shirts,' said Jakob. He went over to his bag and pulled one out, taking care not to dislodge his treasures. Pulling at the shirt, he ripped it into strips and handed them over.

Kizzy spread the paste on Raluca's leg before wrapping it with the torn shirt, tying it into a knot. She stood up and put her hands on her hips. 'There, by tonight the poison should be out.'

'Now eat,' said Herr Engel. Jakob hadn't noticed he'd been cooking while he'd been watching Kizzy.

They all sat and consumed a bread roll and some reheated smoked meat with potatoes. It felt like a feast. Herr Engel even made some hot chocolate.

'Don't expect this every night. Not with three mouths to feed.' Herr Engel stared pointedly at Kizzy. 'Our provisions won't last long.'

Jakob realised how exhausted he looked. The girl – deliberately or not, he wasn't sure – ignored the implication. 'I can always hunt.'

His guardian shook his head before taking the last gulp of his hot chocolate. He stood up. 'Hurry up, we need to rest now. We ride up to the mountains tonight.'

Jakob found a flattish bit of grassy ground. Wrapping his blanket round himself, he lay down. It smelt of horses and tobacco. The others had found their own places to sleep. Looking up to the sky, he watched birds swooping and dancing above him. The farm and the stables seemed a long time ago. He sighed deeply, his eyelids drooping.

Kizzy's quiet voice joined the birdsong. 'Where are we going?'

Chapter 8

Herr Engel shook Jakob. 'Oi, we need to think about making a move. Check Raluca's leg.'

He groaned as he rolled out of his blanket, sleep still sticking his eyes shut. 'What time is it?' he asked.

'About four,' said Herr Engel.

'In the afternoon?'

'Uh huh!'

'Argh, my body's so confused!' Jakob sat with his head in his hands.

His guardian ignored his moaning. 'This way we have time to eat and sort the horses in the daylight.'

Jakob looked across the fire. 'Where's Kizzy?'

Engel followed his gaze. 'How would I know?' He growled, 'Roma never stay anywhere for long. Thought she'd manage at least one day with us though.' He shook his head.

Jakob stretched, trying to click his back into

place. Lying on the ground had been very hard and cold. He'd missed his bed. 'She'll be back.' He walked over to Raluca.

'I'll believe it when I see it.'

The stallion was pleased to see Jakob. He pushed the boy with his head.

'How are you doing?' He rubbed Raluca's neck under his long mane. The hair was still warm and soft. 'Your breathing's a lot calmer. You're even standing properly.' All positive signs, he was sure.

The stallion lifted his front leg.

'Ha! Are you showing me it's better?' He held the leg briefly. 'Steady on, lad, we need to let Herr Engel look at it.'

His guardian undid the bandage. In amongst the herb poultice, there was a lot of pus on the bandages.

'Ewww. That's horrible.'

Herr Engel looked up. 'Better on there than in his leg. Take him to the river and wash the leg, please.'

Jakob led him down into the water and stood in the shallows. The river meandered slowly past them. Raluca lifted the leg again, allowing him to splash cool water over it. He let his hand run down the leg. 'There's no swelling. It seems to have gone down and isn't so hot.' Engel came over to double-check.

'Of course it's fine. Told you it would be.' They looked towards the voice.

Kizzy came along the riverbank carrying three fish and a mass of mushrooms. 'Hungry? I went fishing.'

'Told you,' said Jakob to Herr Engel.

Kizzy looked confused. 'Told him what?'

'Nothing,' said Engel, giving Jakob a look he knew too well. Time to shut up. 'The poultice did a good job. You must teach me what you put in it.'

Kizzy shrugged. 'It's only a few herbs. Shall I get the fish ready?'

Herr Engel moved back towards the fire. 'Yes, you should, now you're back. I'll get this going properly again. Jakob, get more wood when you've finished with Raluca. I want to build it up.'

Jakob led the horse back out of the river and left him to graze. Wandering into the wood, he picked up small logs and twigs. Snapping the longer branches in two, he piled them up in his arms. As he decided to go back, there was the terrifying *chit-chat* of a machine gun.

He raced back to the clearing, expecting the worst. 'Are you all right?' he panted, trying to catch his breath.

Kizzy sat by the river, seemingly unperturbed. 'Yes?' She hung a half-gutted fish in the air. 'You hungry?'

Jakob ignored her question. 'But the gunfire?' He threw the logs down, feeling a little stupid. He knew his face had gone red.

'Stop panicking.' Herr Engel picked up some of the logs and put them on the fire. 'It's a long way off.'

'But it sounded so close.' Jakob moved near to his guardian and whispered, 'I thought it might've been Bauer killing the horses.' He realised as he said it how ridiculous he sounded, but it was too late. The words had fallen out of his mouth.

Herr Engel took hold of Jakob's elbow and led him to one side. 'It's the mountains and the valley,' he whispered. 'They make the sounds roll around: a trick of nature. Forget about Bauer. He'd have found us by now if he wanted to, I'm sure.' He squeezed Jakob's elbow once and walked away, leaving him there, his heart still thumping.

'All right then,' he said quietly.

Kizzy was busy chopping the mushrooms she'd foraged, oblivious.

Jakob shoved his hands into his pockets and went off to check on the horses. Raluca nudged at his arm. He slipped his hand back out and the horse nuzzled it, flicking his tail lightly. The stallion mouthed at the palm of his hand with his soft lips.

'Hello, boy. I miss your mate.' The stallion's ears flicked to and fro as he listened. Jakob's throat was dry, and he swallowed hard. 'I know you're doing your best, but Allegra understood me.'

The horse pushed into him, almost knocking him over.

'Hey, what're you doing?'

The horse did it again.

'All right, I get the message. You *do* understand me. I'll stop whingeing.'

This time Raluca rested his muzzle back on Jakob's hand and blew softly. Jakob laughed.

'Come and eat,' shouted Kizzy. 'It's all done.'

Jakob sat by the fire.

'You all right?' asked Herr Engel.

He felt his face flush again. 'Yes, Raluca told me off.'

'Ah, so you're listening to the horses now. We'll make a horse whisperer of you yet,' laughed his guardian. He handed him a plate. 'Eat!'

Jakob ate quickly, overcome with hunger. Only when he finished did he look up to see Kizzy staring at him strangely.

'Are you really a Jew? Or did you just say that to get me to come here?'

Jakob was taken aback. He looked across at Herr Engel, who shrugged. Sitting up straight, he automatically looked around to make sure no one could hear. 'Yes, I'm Jewish.'

The girl pulled a face. 'You don't behave or look like a Jew.'

Jakob frowned in confusion. 'I can't exactly behave like one anymore, can I, and what are we supposed to look like?' He didn't understand what she was getting at.

'I don't know, but you don't look like it.' She picked at her food.

Herr Engel slapped his leg. 'Daft girl, of course he's a Jew.'

'But you're not.'

His guardian shook his head. 'No, I'm not. So?'

'How come he's here with you?'

Herr Engel leant forward, tapping his coffee mug against his plate. 'It's a long story. Goodness knows how he got to us without being caught. I found him hiding in with Allegra. Normally Allegra would only let me into his stall, but he was quite happy to have this young lad in there. The stallion protected Jakob. I knew he must be a good boy.'

'At the farm?' asked Kizzy.

'No, back in Vienna,' Jakob explained. 'My father's a doctor and my mother worked with him as a nurse. He was putting a plan together for getting us out but things didn't work quickly enough. When the Germans first came, we had to move out of our big apartment in Leopoldstadt into one room. Mother wasn't happy because other people soon moved into our big flat, but at least we were still together. Lots of people weren't.'

'Go on,' said Kizzy. She was like a terrier with a bone. He took a deep breath and poked at the ground with a stick.

'On the 9th of November – I know it was the 9th because it was two days after my seventh birthday – there was trouble outside. We could hear glass being smashed and screaming. The smell of smoke came in through the window, so we all huddled together, until Herr Klein, the bookseller from down the road, came banging on the door. He told my father lots of people were hurt and needed his help. Of course my father didn't hesitate, he always helped people, so he ran out, his coat flying behind him and his bag in his hand. He shouted back at us, "See you in a bit, stay safe." I never saw him again.'

Jakob gulped and paused. He tried to remember what they sounded like. He screwed his eyes shut but their laughter still wouldn't come back to him. The only laughter in his memory now was Herr Engel's, and that was rare.

Kizzy coughed, urging him on. He shook his head.

'It got late and he still hadn't come back and Mother was getting fidgety, pacing around the room. The shouting, screaming and glass smashing were getting far worse. It wasn't long before she grabbed her nurse's bag and ran out too. She promised she'd find him and they'd both be back. She told me not to open the door to anyone. So I hid under my bed, read by torchlight to pass the time, and tried not to hear what was going on outside.' He could feel his heart racing as he remembered. He took a sip of coffee, trying to compose himself. It tasted pretty awful.

'Neither of them came back. I stayed there for a few days, but when the food ran out, and I could hear people being taken away, I panicked.' Jakob took a deep breath, brushing his face with his arm. 'I looked for them but I couldn't find them anywhere. The Nazis seemed to have spirited them away. I didn't know what to do. So I ran to the one place I had always felt safe and happy when my parents had taken me there. I went across the canal to Michaelerplatz and to the Spanish Riding School. I sneaked into the stalls with the horses.'

Herr Engel nodded. 'The Director at the time wasn't too happy initially, but I told him it'd be fine, I'd look after him, and I did. Jakob did odd jobs and worked with the horses, hidden from sight. But it was very dangerous, we nearly got caught several times.'

'Yes, the last time I had to dive into the dung heap to stop being found. It wasn't fun!'

Kizzy half-laughed.

'That's when Director Podhaisk sent us away.

Most people didn't know I was there. At the new place I could really look after the horses.'

Herr Engel interrupted him, 'And do your classes.'

He smiled. 'And do my classes. He's strict about education. I'm the best educated groom around.'

'That's because it's important, that's why,' said his guardian.

Jakob took a last mouthful of food. 'Now do you believe me?'

Kizzy put her head to one side. 'Maybe. Where are your parents?'

Jakob gazed up at the sky. A swallow soared by, free. He shrugged his shoulders. 'No idea. Dead?' What was he supposed to say!

Herr Engel shook his head and got up, touching Jakob's shoulder as he walked by. 'Enough! It's the past. We need to focus on where we're going. Let's pack up. I want to get started as soon as the sun goes down.' He threw the dregs of his coffee on the fire.

Chapter 9

All three of them scrutinised the map.

'Can't we go along there?' asked Kizzy, her finger tracing the line of a road nearby.

'No,' Herr Engel said. 'Too dangerous. I reckon it'll be full of checkpoints.'

'Are you sure?' Kizzy stared straight at Engel.

'No,' Engel barked back. 'But do you, a Roma girl, want to take the risk?' He jabbed his finger at her.

Kizzy looked away. 'I only asked.' She pulled at her sweater. Jakob almost felt sorry for her but not quite.

'Well, don't. Unless you want to take over the planning?'

Her face flamed red. She chewed the side of her nails.

'Right, I'll continue then, shall I?' Herr Engel pointed at the route on the map. 'I think we should try this way. It goes further along the river and then over the mountain, before we dip down the other side. That's where our next resting place is.'

Jakob sighed. It appeared a very long way. The mountains looked pretty insurmountable too. Were they going to be able to do this?

Not wanting to think about it, he concentrated on the map. A town smudged by a crease caught his eye. Should he say something? Herr Engel was already in such a bad mood but…

'Are we following the river again?' he asked.

'For God's sake, yes,' said Herr Engel through gritted teeth. The enormity of it all appeared to weigh heavy on him too. 'Weren't you listening?'

Jakob ploughed on, 'Yes … sorry, it's just … look.' He pointed to the smudge by the river. 'Aren't we going to be a bit close to that town?' He leant in. 'Leizmann?'

Herr Engel peered closely and sighed. 'Oh.' He waved his hand across the map. 'We'll have to work that out when we get nearer.'

Kizzy raised her eyebrows.

His guardian folded the map and tucked it into his saddlebag before tacking up Monte. The stallion swung round, snatching at some sweet grass he'd spotted.

'Ouch, that's my foot! Move over, will you.' Herr Engel leant against the grey and pulled his foot out from underneath his hoof. He grabbed at his boot and hopped around. 'Bloody animal.'

Jakob walked to Raluca and started to tack him up too, keeping well out of the way. Shouldn't they be more worried about that town? But Jakob wasn't going to say anything. Instead he puffed up his cheeks, blowing out all the air in a deep sigh.

'I assume you're all right riding Pluto again?' said Herr Engel to Kizzy.

'Yes, do you want me to lead the others?'

Jakob looked at her. He was torn: part of him knew it would make his life easier if they shared the horses out but, on the other hand, he wanted to prove he could do it. He focused on tightening Raluca's girth.

'Don't be ridiculous, girl,' Herr Engel said. 'You've got no proper bridle or saddle; the stallions will pull you off.'

'I'll be fine,' Kizzy flashed back. 'We can lead three each. It's only fair.'

Herr Engel shook his head. The girl was determined though. His guardian wasn't used to defiance.

84

Kizzy vaulted onto the back of Pluto. 'Hand some over, then.' She held the makeshift rope bridle in one hand and waved the other in the air, demanding attention.

Herr Engel gave her the lead ropes for Flavory and two of his horses, turned to Jakob and barked, 'Hurry up. I want to get going.'

As he handed over the ropes to Jakob, Herr Engel seemed to want to say something. Instead, he walked over to Monte and mounted the stallion.

Herr Engel led the way, Kizzy followed and Jakob made up the rear. All the horses were skittish after their good rest, dancing and prancing. Jakob had a job keeping them all together.

He looked down at Raluca's leg; the stallion seemed to be moving well, no sign of lameness. Jakob felt relieved. He sat deep into the saddle. Allegra and Raluca were very different rides, but he began to enjoy himself. A cool breeze shook the branches above him. The sound of hooves echoed through the wood. It all seemed very calm. Maybe everything would be all right.

'Argh!' shouted Herr Engel. He flew out of his saddle, nearly toppling over his horse's shoulder as Monte planted all four feet solidly on the floor.

Jakob gasped. Raluca's ears went flat back, his eyes rolling. The other stallions careered into Raluca's rump, causing havoc.

'What's the matter?' said Jakob, struggling to hang on to Raluca.

'I don't know,' snapped Herr Engel. 'He just stopped. Come on, you stupid animal, get a move on.'

Monte was going nowhere.

'It's all right. I'll go in front,' volunteered Kizzy. 'Maybe he'll follow me.'

She tried to move Pluto on. He reared up, swivelling around. She lost her grip and had to grab for his mane, but she still slipped off his back, screaming and landing unceremoniously on the ground.

'Are you all right?' shouted Jakob.

'Of course!' She jumped up, very red-faced, brushing the pine needles, leaves and mud off herself. 'What's the matter with them?'

It was chaos. All the stallions who hadn't escaped were desperate to do so. They pulled hard, rearing and bucking, snatching at their bits. Jakob felt sure his shoulders would dislocate at any moment. The horses tossed their heads backwards and whinnied, flashing the whites of their eyes, mouths foaming and necks dark with sweat.

'They're terrified of something.' He sniffed. 'What's that smell?'

A thick, sweet, rotting smell cloyed at the back of his throat.

'I can't see anything; perhaps there's a dead deer nearby.'

'Don't just stand there, girl, catch them.' Herr Engel seemed angrier and angrier with Monte, who swung round and round in an attempt to get away. The horse snorted in fear.

Engel let go of all his other stallions. 'Stupid horse, behave!' he screamed. Then he did something Jakob had never seen him do in the whole time he'd lived with him. He lost his temper with a horse and thumped Monte hard.

Jakob and Kizzy stared at each other.

The stallion bolted back down the path with Engel hanging on to his mane.

'Whoa!' Jakob leant out of his saddle and made a grab for Monte's bridle, catching hold of the reins. He managed to pull the stallion to a halt – just. The horse was frothing at the mouth, terrified.

He couldn't look across at his guardian. 'Wait here,' he said quietly.

Focusing on Monte, he tried to scratch the stallion's forehead. It was almost impossible with all the reins and ropes. 'It's fine, lad. It'll be all right.' The horse remained still, breathing heavily as he watched him cautiously.

'Don't know what all the fuss is about. I'm going back down the path. Bring the others when you've rounded them up,' growled Herr Engel.

Jakob barely nodded at him, swallowing his confusion, before swinging Raluca away from them. He squeezed his legs and pushed the stallion on. 'All right Kizzy, let's round them up. If we take them back down the path they may settle down. Then I'll go up ahead and see what's frightening them.' He twisted round. 'Can you hear that noise? There's a very faint buzzing?'

'Yes,' said Kizzy. 'Maybe that's part of it.'

'Could well be. Let's get these stallions back.'

The loose stallions had moved away from the smell. They mingled among the trees. Grateful they were mainly white horses, Jakob formed a plan.

'Kizzy, lead your stallions to Herr Engel.'

The girl nodded. 'What are you going to do?'

'You'll see.' He smiled.

Kizzy walked back down the path with the three stallions behind her. Jakob watched her go before checking his ropes. 'You ready, boys? We need to get these others moving right away.'

All the horses flicked their ears forward except Jupiter, whose ears were flat back.

'Now Jupiter, don't be difficult.'

The stallion snorted at him.

He turned back in his saddle and squeezed his legs gently so Raluca moved forward into the trees. Up ahead Pluto did exactly what he'd hoped. The rose-grey followed Kizzy down the path. However, Theo, Duo and a grey, Romana, stayed among the trees. If one of Jakob's horses went the wrong side of a trunk, they'd all be in a right knot. He said one of his quiet prayers as he pulled them through the gap. Twigs snatched at his hair and sweater as he raised an arm.

'Hey-yup, come on, boys, off you go. Follow Kizzy, hey-yup.'

The stallions raised their heads and gazed at him, slightly puzzled. Ears twitching, tails swishing, very slowly they moved off until they were all trotting back on the path, heading towards the girl.

It seemed like it took forever. Kizzy had the sense to stop and wait for the stallions to come to her. Slowly, one by one, they did, and nuzzled her hand. Thank goodness, thought Jakob, his head pounding. It'd been exhausting and thirsty work. When he caught up with Kizzy, he smiled. 'We did it!'

They led all the stallions back to the waiting Herr Engel. He handed them some bread and water.

'Right, I think you and I should go and see. Kizzy, you stay with the horses.'

Jakob thought Kizzy would object so he gave her a look. Her mouth was sullen. 'Don't be too long.' She looked around. 'I don't like it here.'

Jakob was surprised. He thought she would be perfectly all right in the woods. He wondered why. When Herr Engel wasn't looking, he winked at her. She nodded but didn't return his smile.

Jakob and his guardian left Kizzy soothing the horses as they walked back down the path.

'What do you think it is?' asked Jakob as they trudged along.

Herr Engel stared straight ahead. 'I think Kizzy may be right, a dead deer or something.' He hesitated. 'Look, about earlier…'

Jakob didn't want to hear it. He cut straight through his words. 'It doesn't matter.'

Herr Engel looked away. They carried on in silence.

It didn't take long to get to the place where the horses had refused to go on.

'When we get this sorted, we must plan how to get past the town you spotted.'

Jakob glanced at him. Was that Herr Engel admitting the town was a problem? Puffing out his cheeks, his lips vibrated as he blew out.

'You all right?' Engel asked.

He nodded. 'There's the smell again.'

'And that dull noise. What on earth is it?'

'It's coming from over there.' They wandered towards it. As they got closer, they both put their hands over their nose and mouth. The smell was putrid. They gagged. The buzzing noise got louder too. The clouds parted and the full moon came out. It was so bright it was almost daylight. Ahead was a pile of freshly dug earth.

His guardian clambered up first. Stopping abruptly, he put his hand up. 'Don't...'

Herr Engel gulped. Vomit sprayed across the ground. He turned to Jakob, wiping his mouth. All the colour had drained from his face. 'Get away. Don't look!' he screamed, pushing him back down the hill. But Jakob had already seen something.

'There are horses?' He'd never seen Herr Engel like this. 'People too?'

'We need to get away,' said Engel, dragging Jakob. A cloud of flies flew up behind them.

'I don't understand.' His chest felt like it would burst. He couldn't keep up with his guardian as he ran.

'It's full of bodies, you mustn't look.'

They tumbled back down to the path, running and gasping for air.

Chapter 10

When they reached the clearing, Kizzy glanced up from the stallions. For the first time, she looked to Jakob so small and vulnerable. A lump lodged in his throat. He swallowed hard.

'It was bad, wasn't it?' She twisted one of the ropes round and round her hand. 'I heard you scream. I didn't know what to do.' Her face was grey.

Jakob couldn't speak.

Herr Engel told her. 'There were lots of bodies. I've never seen anything like it. Men, women, children, babies. That's what they smelt.'

'And horses, I saw horses,' said Jakob.

'Yes, and horses.' Herr Engel's voice was barely a whisper now.

Kizzy buried her head in Pluto's neck. 'I'm sorry.'

Herr Engel rested his hand on her shoulder. 'Why sorry? It's not your fault. You needn't apologise for those monsters.' He kicked out at a random log, before turning back to them. 'But we need to work out how to get these horses past it.'

Kizzy spoke into Pluto's neck, her voice barely a whisper. 'Is there another route we could take?'

Jakob waited for his guardian to explode at being challenged but Herr Engel sounded resigned and gentle. 'No. Remember what I said: this is the only path.'

Jakob finally found his voice again. 'How about we lead them? Maybe talking to them all the time so they focus on us.'

His guardian nodded. 'That might work. You can go first. We better wrap something round our faces to avoid the smell.'

It sounded so easy. They took hold of their horses and slowly moved back along the path. Jakob held the ropes for Raluca, Maestro, Largo and Jupiter in his hands.

'Right, Maestro.' He looked up at the stallion and his neck cricked. 'You are so tall! We really need your Sunday's child luck here.'

Jupiter snatched the ropes and yanked on them.

'Will you stop doing that?' He tried to pull the

rope free. The gentle black Maestro pushed Jupiter's muzzle away. Raluca did the same from the other side. Jakob couldn't help but smile at the bossy stallions.

'Well, Jupiter, your friends are telling you how to behave. Largo, just you now, you need to keep up with us.'

The flea-bitten grey was dawdling along, his head down, snuffling for grass. Jakob pulled at his rope too. 'Come on, my boys, off we go. We can do this, can't we?'

He clicked his tongue. The crunch of hooves echoed around the forest again. An owl hooted in the distance. 'I know you will smell something really horrible in a minute but you've got to trust me. I won't let anything happen to you.'

When they got near to where Monte had stopped before, Jakob talked more, nonsense words, anything that came into his head. He turned round, facing the horses, hoping that it would distract them but their ears twitched, then their nostrils flared. He knew they smelt the rotting flesh. He tried to be as soothing as possible.

'It's all right, boys.'

But Raluca struck at the floor with his front leg.

He wouldn't move. When Jakob pulled, the horse reared up. White froth collected by his bit again. They were all showing the whites of their eyes.

He put his arms up. 'Whoa, boys, whoa!' Jakob moved them backwards. He didn't want to lose control and have to round them back up. His shoulders slumped. He shouted to the others, 'It's not working. Go back. We need to think of an alternative.' Jakob rejoined Kizzy and his guardian and sat down heavily on a log.

Herr Engel sat next to him and put his head in his hands. 'I can't see how we can do it. Maybe we should go back to the farm and take the risk.'

Jakob looked across at Kizzy, who shrugged her shoulders. But he wasn't having any of it. 'No. Come on. You told me it was all about the horses. We can find a solution. I'm not giving up and you're not either.' He rested his hand briefly on Herr Engel's shoulder.

Suddenly a mad idea slipped into Jakob's head. 'Kizzy, are any of your herbs really smelly?'

Kizzy stared at him blankly. Slowly she realised what he was thinking and a smile crept across her face. 'Yes, yes, some are! Wait here, I'll find them.' She handed her horses over to Jakob and ran off.

A quarter of an hour later Kizzy re-emerged from the wood carrying various herbs and bits of greenery.

'What are those?'

'This and that, mostly wild garlic.' Kizzy asked Jakob, 'Can you find me a big stone? I need to grind them together.'

Herr Engel glanced up from the log. You could almost see the lightbulb switch on inside him as a broad smile stretched across his face. 'Ah, that is clever!'

Jakob found a stone and for the next ten minutes Kizzy ground the herbs and weeds together. The smell was strong but not unpleasant.

Once the paste was ready, Kizzy smeared a little under the nostrils of each horse. They tossed their heads around but soon settled. The inquisitive Pluto came over, nudging the bowl out of Kizzy's hands. What was left in the bowl went all over the front of her sweater.

Jakob laughed 'You stink! Can I have a bit, too?' He scraped some off her sweater and smeared it on his top lip. The smell was powerful but not as bad as death. 'It works, you should do it.' He passed a bit to Herr Engel.

Kizzy grinned. 'I don't think I need to, my sweater is strong enough, thanks to Pluto!'

All three gazed around at the horses. They couldn't help but laugh at the animals with their green moustaches.

'Don't know what you're laughing at? Have you seen yourselves?' said Herr Engel, smiling. 'Right, let's try again.'

Jakob went first, talking to the horses all the while. 'All right, boys, you look silly but if it works it'll be worth it.'

When they got to where Monte had refused to move, Jakob watched Raluca. His ears flicked to and fro but he kept moving – tentatively. 'This is it, boys, we can do it. One more step, just one more step.'

He could see the pile of earth to his right. The buzz of flies was horrendous. Talk louder, thought Jakob.

'Keep looking at me, boys. Don't look over there, you don't want to see it.' He kept chattering about everything and nothing as they made their way along the path.

They took more than an hour to get all the horses far enough away from the dead bodies for them to relax. Jakob saw the tension in Raluca's body melt away the further they travelled.

Herr Engel finally shouted, 'I think we can mount up again. We need to ride fast to make up time.'

All three felt exhausted. Relieved, they got back into the saddle and headed off, picking up speed.

Chapter 11

Up ahead the forest thinned. The river moved faster, tumbling over rocks.

'Herr Engel, what are we going to do about Leizmann?'

His guardian looked back at him. 'I'm not sure. Do we know how far it is?'

Jakob shrugged. 'A bit further, I think. Why don't we stop and give the horses a drink? We could look at the map then.'

Herr Engel said nothing but reined Monte back. Jakob assumed this meant his idea had been a good one. His guardian slipped off Monte's back.

'Let them drink their fill. Hopefully that'll get rid of the paste. If not, wash it off. Better wipe it off our faces too.'

The horses stood in the shallows of the river and drank, long and full.

'Right, let's see where we are.' Herr Engel

unfolded the map. He lit his torch. It flickered. 'No! The batteries must be going.'

'Save it,' said Kizzy. 'I've got a candle.'

She smacked a flint and steel together several times before a spark caught, lighting the candle from the taper.

'Give it here,' Herr Engel asked, lighting his cigarette from it too. He puffed at it and the tip glowed in the dark. 'Saves my matches!'

With the gentle glow of the candle, they peered at the map.

'Look,' said Jakob, 'the forest ends before the town and the river goes virtually right through it. How are we going to get by without being seen?'

Engel sighed. 'Perhaps we should take this detour.' He used his cigarette to show another route.

Kizzy watched his hand. 'That seems miles out of the way and crosses many roads. You said there might be checkpoints. Do you think we'll be safe?'

Herr Engel rubbed his face with both hands. 'I wish I could promise that.'

Jakob sat back on his haunches. 'And that pit might as well have been a message from Bauer. Plus, we can't afford the time, can we? It seems to take us the wrong side of the mountains.' He tilted his head to one side, wondering whether Herr Engel would be angry with him for challenging him.

Kizzy frowned, puzzled. 'What?' Jakob saw she was irritated. She snapped, 'Look, why are you so worried about Bauer?'

'The dead horses and people in the pit. I thought maybe they were a personal message to us.' The words had slipped out of Jakob's mouth before he could stop them.

The colour drained from her face. She gulped. 'I … I doubt you need to worry about him. He was unconscious for ages. I watched for as long as I dared before I caught Pluto. He didn't come round. And even when he did, I doubt he'd remember anything.' She picked at some twigs on the floor. 'I was there a while before you got there too. I took a wild guess that you'd be avoiding the roads, so that was the only way you could go. I waited as I thought I could warn you if there was going to be trouble. I saw that he was really drunk. He'd already had a blazing row with one of the other officers. They don't seem to like him at all.'

Herr Engel and Jakob smiled with relief. Perhaps that solved one problem, but not the one they were now facing. Jakob looked back at the map. He had another idea.

'Why don't I go into the town and check it out?' He pointed to where he meant on the map. 'If we ride to this clearing, we could hide up there with the horses. It's not far from the road. I could follow it into the town. See?' He looked up at the others. Kizzy seemed dubious but Herr Engel nodded. 'If I can get in there I can see if the map is wrong.'

Kizzy piped up. 'I'll come with you. I'm used to moving around without being caught. I've done it for many months now.'

Herr Engel laughed, 'We saw you.'

The girl pushed at the ground with her foot. She seemed offended. 'Only when I meant you to. I'd been watching you for ages before that. I just wanted to be near the horses.'

He patted her on her back and half smiled. 'I know.' He looked at Jakob. 'She's right. She'll help you. We need to get going. I reckon that clearing's about half an hour away.'

They rode quickly and quietly through the

forest. This clearing was different from the others. There was an abandoned barn, built of stone and wood, in the centre. It looked like a carcass with its ribcage stretched across the roof.

'A bit of luxury tonight,' said Kizzy.

Engel stared hard at her, whispering, 'Ssh, will you? Wait here while I check it out.'

She sighed loudly as Herr Engel trotted ahead. When he had searched round, he put his thumbs up.

Jakob moved into the barn and untacked the stallions. A damp, disused smell hung in the air. 'You all right, Raluca?' He began to rub him down but Herr Engel stopped him.

'I'll do the horses. You go into town. The sooner you go the better.'

'All right. Come on, Kizzy.' Jakob grabbed her arm. 'And keep quiet.'

The children travelled quickly through the forest, not far from the road, keeping low to the ground. Branches snatched at their faces. Brambles tried to trip them up. They kept moving as quietly as they could, following the twists and turns of the river.

As the trees got thinner, Kizzy slipped in front and led the way. It was nearly an hour before they could see the town ahead. Swerving in and out of the shadows until they reached the edge of the forest, they both sat on their haunches, breathing heavily, and watched the houses in the distance. A motorbike roared along the road, climbing up the mountain and into the town centre. In the darkness they saw the outline of numerous buildings. Many had lots of narrow windows, others had turrets. Tall spires pierced the sky. Jakob thought it looked straight out of a storybook as the moon shone down.

'It's very dark,' said Jakob.

'Blackout, of course. That's when towns are at their most dangerous, when the soldiers are around and are twitchy,' whispered Kizzy. She nodded towards the forest. 'Let's keep close. We need to see where the river goes.'

Jakob nodded. The bank dipped right down and the water was very shallow and slow running.

Crouching low, they crept along the edge of the forest. The clouds had covered the moon now, it was pitch black. They could hear bats swooping and diving above them.

'Get off, will you,' she whispered, pulling her hand out from under Jakob's foot for the third time.

'Sorry. Shall I go first? I won't tread on you then.'

'No, that won't work.' Kizzy grabbed hold of Jakob's hand. 'Come this way. Keep low.'

She led him up to the side of a building. 'Keep flat against the wall and follow me.'

He felt like a bumbling fool next to her as she slipped in and out of the shadows, dragging him along. He realised she was right. She knew exactly how to disappear.

'Say nothing. Do whatever I do.'

She didn't give him a chance to respond. Instead she moved silently, flat against the rough wall along an alleyway. It opened out onto a square and they heard loud voices. Jakob's gut twisted. On one side there was a bar full of Germans. The SS were there, in their grey-green uniforms, talking loudly. Jakob shivered. There were even some Gestapo, similarly dressed, but more dangerous with their police-patterned shoulder flashes edged in poison green. Quietly the Gestapo watched everyone, nonchalant-seeming but taking everything in. Glamorously dressed women draped themselves over the soldiers' arms. Tinkling laughter echoed round the square. They seemed to be the only people around.

Two of the SS soldiers rolled out of the bar, tucking their shirts into their trousers before doing up their uniforms, pushing each other and guffawing. Jakob felt Kizzy tense. She nodded towards the centre of the square, where an old man shuffled past.

'What's he doing out at night?' Kizzy hissed.

Jakob whispered into her hair, 'I don't know. I wish he wasn't.'

The two children weren't the only ones to spot him. The soldiers went over, circling him, barking like dogs. The old man pulled his arms up over his face.

They couldn't hear what the men were saying, but it wasn't good. They pushed the old man between them, like he was a toy, spinning him round and round. Everyone in the bar cheered them on. Kizzy gripped Jakob's hand.

One soldier barked a question at the old man. He obviously didn't like his answer as he took out his pistol and whipped him with it until he was on the floor, bleeding. Jakob moved forward.

'No,' Kizzy gasped, pulling him back against the rough wall. 'You'll get us killed.'

'But … we can't just stand here.'

The look on her face told him that's exactly what they would do. He felt sick.

Before they could say or do anymore, a gunshot rang out across the square. The old man twitched, then was still. An ugly silence hung in the air, broken by a cacophony of laughter and clapping from the bar. The soldiers spun round and did an extravagant bow.

'Pigs,' Jakob muttered under his breath. He slumped against the wall, slipping down until he squatted.

Kizzy grabbed his arm. 'We need to get to that river.' He saw her peer across the square. 'Come on, we must get a move on.'

They soon found themselves by a bridge. There was a road leading to it and two paths branching off on either side, running alongside the river. Lining the road and the paths were many buildings. In the dark, Jakob couldn't work out what sort of places they were, or who might be hiding inside. A wave of nausea swept over him.

'Are you all right?' asked Kizzy.

He gathered his thoughts. 'Yes.' He grabbed her hand. 'Let's go along here.' He pulled her along the path to the left, slightly away from the bridge. 'Can you see the river?'

'No, not yet.' She looked over the waist-high wall along the path.

He leant right over the wall. The river rolled under the bridge a good five metres beneath. The bridge joined one part of the town to another further up the mountain.

'Kizzy, see, it's right down there. It's cut a ravine.' She leaned further to see what he was seeing.

'There are no proper banks to ride on.' She slumped backwards. 'We must take the other route with all the checkpoints.' She sounded so defeated and despondent.

Jakob reached right over the wall so his feet weren't touching the floor. 'No, I reckon we can ride straight through the town. Look, the river isn't deep and if we go when it's dark, we'll be so far down no one will see us.'

He glanced up to read Kizzy's face. Instead he saw something that made his blood turn to ice.

A faint light glowed on the bridge. It was a cigarette. It moved towards them. He grabbed Kizzy round the waist, throwing her flat on the floor. Instinctively she tried to scream, but he put his hand over her mouth, pushing them both close against the wall. 'Ssh,' he begged.

He could hear the heavy footsteps of a patrol echoing around them as they reached the end of the bridge.

Please don't come down the path. Jakob squeezed his eyes tight shut and clenched every muscle. *Please God. I beg you. Not this way. Not now.* A breeze ruffled their hair.

'Can you smell garlic?' asked a faint disconnected voice.

Jakob opened his eyes and gasped. 'The paste!' he whispered into Kizzy's hair. She nodded, her eyes wide with panic. He pulled her close.

Another voice sneered. 'You're such a city boy. It's just the wild garlic from the riverbank. There's loads of it at this time of year. Now hurry up, I'm cold. Let's get a move on.'

Kizzy's hair smelt of the woods. Jakob glanced to the side just as the glowing butt of a cigarette fell so close to them, it nearly touched his hand. He held his breath. Would the soldiers follow their cigarette? He waited for a hand on his shoulder to drag him away. It never came. The voices and footsteps disappeared.

'That was close!' he said into Kizzy's shoulder. He let out a long sigh of relief. 'They've gone. Come on, quick. Let's get back.'

Chapter 12

Back with Herr Engel and the horses, Jakob tried to describe his plan. His guardian scratched his head.

'Ride straight through the town – that's pretty audacious.'

They stared at the map.

Jakob felt disappointment build in his stomach. 'I know it's crazy but it'll take forever the other way, and it's full of checkpoints.' Herr Engel stroked his beard. Kizzy stood to one side, watching and patting Pluto's neck. Silence enveloped them all. After a few long moments, Herr Engel spoke.

'You really think it'll work?'

Jakob nodded.

Kizzy half smiled at Jakob. 'It sounds mad, but I think he's right. It gets us a long way up the mountain too. Anything that cuts our journey must be good for the horses and probably safer. The Nazis are everywhere. We saw…'

Her voice trailed away. Jakob knew she was remembering the old man.

Herr Engel walked away. Jakob waited. His guardian swivelled on his heels and marched back.

'Right, the question is, do we go now? Or shall we wait until tomorrow night? It's nearly four a.m. already.' Herr Engel peered at the map. 'My next planned stop is here.' He pointed at a place on the other side of the mountain.

Jakob leant over the map too. 'I reckon it'll take us half an hour's riding to get to the town. Give us another half hour to get clear through to the other side, because we won't be able to go fast. How long will it take us to get over the mountain?'

'A lot longer than that.'

Kizzy sat down with a thump on a broken wall. 'I'm so tired.'

Jakob was exhausted too. The adrenalin high of outwitting the patrol had disappeared. 'Will we be safe here?' He gazed round the barn.

'Yes, I think we should be. As long as we don't light a fire during the day so there's no smoke for people to notice. And we must keep the noise down.' He looked pointedly at Kizzy. 'Luckily I've cooked some food already. I thought you might be hungry. And looking at the state of you two, I think we definitely rest here and leave tomorrow night. It wouldn't hurt the horses to take it easy for a day either.'

They ate with relish the potatoes and the small amount of smoked meat Herr Engel had managed to save. Jakob realised how hungry he was, scooping up every last mouthful.

'Now, make sure the horses are settled. And that the fire is out and not smouldering.'

The three fed and watered the horses, leaving them corralled in the small patch of land between the barn and the river, before they all lay down inside.

Jakob looked up through the ribs where the roof should have been. The clouds had gone and he could see the stars twinkling away. A shooting star zoomed across the sky, leaving a trail behind it.

'Did you see that?' said Herr Engel. 'A lucky sign.'

Kizzy leaned on her elbow. 'We're supposed to make a wish, aren't we?'

'Think I've used up all my wishes tonight.' Jakob yawned, then remembered earlier when they were in the forest. 'Kizzy, what was wrong in those woods? You never seemed to have a problem before? Why didn't you want to be left on your own?'

He heard her sigh. There was a slight catch to her voice he'd never heard before. 'I'm usually all right.'

Jakob felt he'd asked her something he shouldn't. 'You don't have to say anything. Sorry.'

She sat up. 'No, you and Herr Engel should know.'

Jakob's guardian moved in his bed but said nothing.

'The clearing we were in brought back lots of memories. It was just like the one I was in when the SS came.' Her voice dropped to a hoarse whisper, and she wrapped her arms round herself, holding on tight. 'My pa had seen them coming and told me to climb up a tree as far as I could. Everyone else had gone from the camp the day before, but Pa had promised someone he'd finish a job, so said we'd catch up. We never did.' Kizzy swallowed a sob. 'The SS don't like Roma. They came with their jackboots, kicking over everything in the camp.' Her lips trembled. 'They dragged Ma out of the caravan by her hair. My brother, Bo, tried to run, but they grabbed him, too, and my pa.' Her hands shook as she roughly wiped away snot and tears.

Jakob couldn't listen anymore. He shot out of his bed and sat by her. He wasn't sure whether to put his arm round her or not. Very quietly he said, 'Stop, Kizzy, you don't have to remember. You don't have to tell me. I'm sorry I asked you.'

Her eyes were dark pools. The pain in them made the ache in his heart twist a notch tighter.

'They killed them eventually, but I saw what they did to them before that. It should have been me too. It was only because of the leaves on the tree and my pa sending me up there that it wasn't. That was two, maybe three winters ago.'

This time Jakob did put his arm round her. He knew no words could make it right. Instead he held her thin body tight until she fell asleep in his arms.

'Jakob, wake up.' Somebody was shaking him. It was Kizzy. 'Be quiet, someone will hear you.'

Jakob dragged himself back to reality, away from the nightmare. His shirt was stuck to his body with sweat. He couldn't stop shaking. 'What's happening? I'm so cold,' he stuttered.

'Are you all right? You were screaming. Shall I hold you to keep you warm?'

Jakob nodded, too embarrassed to speak. She pulled the blankets over them both. He felt her warmth through their clothes. Jakob didn't want to look at her. Instead he focused on Raluca. The stallion sensed him watching. The horse stopped grazing and looked towards him, nickering quietly.

In the dim light of the dawn, Kizzy's voice cracked. 'I'm scared.'

The sound of someone moving around the camp woke Jakob with a start. Herr Engel was wandering around in the sunlight. Kizzy was still sound asleep.

'Are you all right, you look like you've seen a ghost?' his guardian asked.

'Yes, I just thought…'

'Oh, you and your thinking. I've told you before about that. Come and help me get ready. Do you want some bread to eat?'

Jakob levered himself out from under Kizzy's arms and joined Herr Engel at the edge of the barn. They watched the horses grazing as they munched their bread. It was a bit dry and stale but Jakob knew better than to complain. Even with all the shortages and rationing they'd always been lucky to have the food they'd had, and he knew it. Herr Engel had always been resourceful.

'Do you want to talk about last night?'

Jakob shook his head then ripped another chunk off the bread. He certainly didn't want to talk about his dream. It had been the old man, mingled in with images of his parents shot in the forehead just like Allegra. His body shuddered at the thought.

Herr Engel stared hard at him then shrugged. 'All right, I'm here if you do.' He changed the subject. 'We can't eat properly until it's dark, when I can light a fire again. We are too far away from any houses for them to see the flames at night, if we keep it small, but they can see smoke during daylight from kilometres away. I think we should leave between ten-thirty and eleven-thirty. That should get us to the town by about midnight. Less dangerous, don't you think?'

Jakob nodded. He looked down. 'I hope it works.'

'It won't be for the lack of trying.' His guardian squeezed his shoulder.

Kizzy stretched and yawned loudly as she came to.

'About time you woke up,' said Herr Engel.

'Harrumph! It's too early.' She pulled on a sweater. Jakob watched as she went over to the river and splashed her face. Clouds of gnats swarmed round her. Someone appeared to have woken up in a very bad mood!

'There's some bread and water here to eat.'

'Is that all?' snapped Kizzy.

'Yes, for the moment. We can't risk a fire until tonight.' Herr Engel glared at her. 'When you've finished, wash the plates we forgot to do last night.' He pointed at Jakob. 'You can set the fire ready for later.'

Kizzy bristled. 'Why doesn't he get the dishes?'

Herr Engel looked surprised.

She said, 'I'm good at fires.'

Jakob sighed and quietly grabbed the plates, walking towards the river. 'You do the fire, I'll do these.'

He knelt and let the flowing water rinse off the plates. It was so cold. He watched a leaf flow down, drifting away from him. He wished he could have got down to the river last night to see how deep it was. Did it run fast or not? Relying on his gut feeling was risky, he knew. A wave of nausea overwhelmed him. He splashed water on his face, hoping to stop it.

'You better do the fire then, hadn't you?' Herr Engel spoke sternly to Kizzy. Jakob felt the chill in his words. It wouldn't make the journey any easier if there was tension between them all.

Taking up one plate, he scooped up river water and in one easy movement he flicked the water towards Kizzy. It arched in a sparkling rainbow before drowning her as she stood near the pile of kindling.

She looked up, water dripping down her face and hair. For a moment Jakob thought maybe he'd done the wrong thing, but then her face cracked and she roared with laughter.

'I'll get you.' She ran towards the river squealing and kicked water at him. They splashed and laughed.

Herr Engel's face was like thunder. 'Ssh, someone'll hear you.'

Kizzy kicked a huge wave of water at him. He stood there, dripping from head to foot. Jakob thought Engel would explode. He held his breath as his guardian moved towards them. Kizzy stood watching, waiting.

Suddenly his face changed. 'Get her legs,' he shouted, running forward and grabbing Kizzy's arms. Jakob did as he was told. Kizzy squealed and thrashed.

'One, two, three…'

Crack!

All three stopped.

'What's that?' whispered Jakob, his heart pounding.

'It sounded like people in the wood over there.' Herr Engel pointed towards the right. 'You gather the horses together as quietly as you can. I'll see if I can see anything.'

Jakob and Kizzy edged over to the horses. He could see his guardian swinging round the outskirts of the camp. The noises were getting louder. Kizzy looked panicked. They were in trouble. Jakob grabbed Raluca's halter and waited. The air stilled.

A herd of deer darted into the camp, jumping the fence into the corral. The startled stallion tossed his head in the air, jarring Jakob's shoulder.

The deer stopped, ears and noses twitching, before sprinting off in every direction, clattering past the horses and back into the wood.

Raluca danced around snorting.

Herr Engel leant against a tree, wiping his forehead, looking shaken. 'Come on, we'd better change clothes and prepare. We mightn't be so lucky next time.'

The mood in the camp was subdued. When Kizzy stripped off, Jakob noticed she was trembling.

'Are you all right?' he whispered.

'Of course, why wouldn't I be?' She stalked off towards Pluto.

Jakob shrugged his shoulders.

Chapter 13

They began the next part of their journey just after eleven. Even though Jakob felt a lot safer in the dark, there was a large knot in his stomach. What if he'd got this all wrong?

Twenty minutes later and closer to the town, Herr Engel slowed all the horses down and signalled to him. 'You can lead the way now. You know how to get to the town via the river.'

Kizzy looked at him expectantly. The enormity of his plan weighed heavy. He gulped.

He steered Raluca towards the dip in the riverbank he'd spotted the night before. 'This is a safe, shallow way into the river. Follow me.'

'I hope you're bloody right.'

Herr Engel's comment did not help Jakob's nerves. He felt sweat trickle down his back, even while he was shivering with cold.

The stallion slowed and peered at the water. Jakob felt him tense. 'Don't worry, it'll be fine. In you go, Raluca!' He squeezed his legs while clicking his tongue. 'Come on, boys, don't let me down,' he muttered. He pulled gently on the ropes and the other stallions followed, stepping tentatively into the river too.

He glanced back at Herr Engel and Kizzy. 'It's all right. It really is quite shallow. We're ahead of the rocks and the fast-running water. It should be okay.' He tried to sound reassuring.

Kizzy looked at Herr Engel then pushed Pluto forward into the river. Engel half laughed and followed.

The sound of splashing hooves seemed to echo around them. Jakob kept his eyes focused on the river, trying to plan every move.

Looking up, he saw the blind bend ahead. The river seemed to flow slowly and wasn't deep, just as he'd thought. He kept Raluca as near to the bank as he could but had to remember he had Maestro, Largo and Jupiter behind him. If he glanced up, he saw the mountains looming, their target for the night. But nearer, and more frighteningly, he saw occasional lights twinkling above them. The indistinct shapes of Leizmann's buildings crawled up the mountain. The spires stood guard ahead and off to the left. With luck, no one would look at the river tonight.

'We can do this, boys,' he whispered.

The water flowed straight down from the snow-capped mountains and was freezing. When it splashed his legs, Jakob gasped. It was up to Raluca's knees now. The stallion lifted his legs high and placed them carefully with every move. The going was slow but not as slow as Jakob had anticipated. They soon reached the other side of the bend. Up ahead he saw the bridge where they'd been the night before. Now they were well-hidden as the banks of the river were several metres high. Nobody could see them unless they peered right over the walls, like they had last night.

He turned to the others, murmuring, 'Are you all right?'

'Blooming wet again,' muttered Herr Engel.

Jakob saw a flash of white. Kizzy must have smiled. She whispered, 'Stop moaning!'

They moved closer and closer to the bridge. Jakob breathed a sigh of relief, then he heard a thundering noise. He looked up to the sky. It wasn't planes.

Kizzy knew the answer. 'Tanks! We need to get under the bridge fast. It must be a convoy. Quick.'

They all stopped worrying about being careful and quiet. They pushed their horses on through the water to the bridge. The stallions were splashing everywhere just as the first tank trundled high above them. Luckily there was enough space for all the horses underneath. The deafening sound echoed around them as the tanks' tracks squealed and thudded above. Engines roared. Bits of stone and debris rained down. The horses started to panic.

'We can't move. We'll be seen,' shouted Jakob.

Raluca reared up as a stone struck him on the head. Jakob held on tight, gripping onto the other horses too. 'It's all right, Raluca. It's only stupid tanks, they can't hurt you,' he lied.

The stallion whinnied loudly before landing back down, pawing at the water, snorting. The others joined in, eyes rolling, ears flicked forward, listening for threats. Terrified, they all danced on their toes.

Jakob looked round. Everyone was having as much trouble as him. After Monte had bucked once more, Herr Engel shouted, 'Get off and hold them close. Keep talking to them. We mustn't let them run. It's too dangerous.'

Jakob slid off Raluca's back and pulled all four horses together. He gasped as the icy water lapped round his thighs. 'S'all right, you're safe. I won't let anything happen to you,' he said over and over again. He took it in turns to stroke and scratch each stallion, breathing onto their muzzles, slowly and evenly. Their eyes were wild at first, but the more he did this the calmer they got, despite the noise still thundering above them.

Chapter 14

Kizzy shouted across, 'How many more can there be?'

It lasted for half an hour before silence descended. They were soaked to the skin and shivering.

'Let's leave it a few minutes before we move off,' said Herr Engel as he mounted Monte.

'I'm sorry,' said Jakob, feeling very shaken.

Herr Engel looked at him, a brief flash of anger in his eyes, 'What for? Like you'd planned for this.' He shook his head. 'You were right; this is the best way. Stop feeling sorry for yourself and lead us up that mountain. You've done a good job.'

Jakob nodded and led the horses away from the bridge, along the river. They splashed their way through the clear, cold water as they headed past the rest of the town. Jakob kept an eye on the banks, but no one seemed to spot them. It took about twenty minutes before the buildings started to disappear and the welcoming safety of the trees and the forest became more obvious.

Jakob sighed with relief: so far so good. They'd done it; they'd got through the town. Now on to the next stage. Up ahead he could see another dip in the riverbank.

'Follow me, there's a way out over here,' he whispered to the others. He pushed Raluca on. 'We'll soon be out of this cold water, boy.'

They all clattered out of the river and up the bank, water, stones and mud flying everywhere. Once they were all on dry land, Jakob asked, 'Should we stop?' praying that Herr Engel would say yes. He was freezing. His teeth were chattering and he couldn't stop shivering.

'No, not yet, we need to get away from here, in case anyone spotted us.'

'Can we trot now, though? I'm so cold,' said Kizzy.

'Definitely! It'll warm you up.' Herr Engel led the way again and pushed Monte into trot.

The terrain rapidly got steeper and the trees were sparser now. There were no branches snatching at their hair and faces anymore. The grass gave way to shingle under hoof.

His guardian shouted, 'Be careful! We need to walk. Too easy for them to lose their footing otherwise.'

Jakob looked back at the town below and could see in the distance the terrifying tanks wending their way further along the road into the distance.

Herr Engel swung round in his saddle. 'We will skirt round the mountain. If we go up any further we'll get caught in the snow line. Much too dangerous and definitely too cold!'

'Thank goodness!' said Jakob. His wet clothes had dried on him and he felt chilled to the bone. 'Do you think they can see us?'

'Hopefully they're too busy with the Allied armies to care about a few horses,' Herr Engel shouted back. 'Let's keep moving. Not too much further to go. We're well over halfway there now.'

Kizzy cheered and punched at the sky with her spare hand. The stallions danced behind her.

Jakob relaxed into his saddle. Above him the Milky Way stretched into the distance, beautiful, even clearer than the night before. He opened his mouth to say something to Kizzy, but the words caught in his throat. She'd only laugh at him. Instead he focused on the route ahead.

There was rarely a word spoken between them for the next few hours. Everyone was too tired and hungry and Jakob could tell the horses were exhausted too. They slogged their way on and on, slowly round the mountain slopes to the other side, then headed down again towards more thick forest. The Milky Way melted away, and the sun stretched its arms upwards, peeping above the horizon. The dawn chorus woke in the wood below them. Jakob felt a palpable sense of relief flow between them all. Kizzy even started singing. He knew they were through the worst of it now.

Relaxing, he let Raluca's reins hang loose and slipped his feet out of the stirrups. His legs dangling down, Jakob leant back in the saddle. The stallion felt sure-footed, until suddenly the scree slipped beneath him. Raluca stumbled and fell to his knees, throwing Jakob forward, jarring his whole body.

'Whoa! Are you all right, boy?' He grabbed the reins and pushed himself back into the saddle, his feet into the irons.

Raluca lurched back up slowly, before continuing to walk on, shaking his head. His skin was twitching.

'You didn't like that much, did you?' Jakob leant forward and rubbed the horse's neck. He called to the others, 'Watch the rocks, they're slippery.'

'Will do,' they shouted. Jakob paid a lot more attention now as he descended the mountain, watching every step.

Herr Engel wasn't so lucky. Jakob jolted when Raluca shied to one side, snatching at the bit, pulling the reins out of his hands, as the peace of the early morning was shattered by a crash. The shingle tumbled down the mountain and, with it, Herr Engel and Monte.

'No! Herr Engel!' Jakob shouted, grabbing hold of the reins again and gripping tightly to Raluca's mane. The horror of what he was watching swept over him. Horse and rider toppled down the mountain, rolling

over

and over

and over.

The screams of both the horse and Herr Engel seared Jakob's heart. He could see that as Engel fell, he'd had the sense to let go of the other horses' ropes. They were sliding on their haunches behind the plummeting man and horse.

They stayed upright … just.

Kizzy let out an ear-splitting wail as she watched the carnage.

'Hold tight onto Pluto and the others, you don't want to follow,' Jakob shouted at her as he gripped onto his own horses. He tried not to think of the noise they were making. Would someone hear them?

He reined Raluca back the whole time, despite being desperate to get down the mountain to Herr Engel. Jakob knew he had to stay in control or they'd all fall. His horses sensed the panic in the air. He turned Raluca round, taking a longer slower route, avoiding all the slipping shingle.

Jakob held his breath as he looked down. Monte and Herr Engel had plummeted all the way down the side, stopping only where the shingle merged into grass. They both lay in a crumpled heap on the scree. Neither was moving.

Up above, eagles circled.

Chapter 15

'Please be all right.' Jakob prayed. He and Kizzy tentatively guided their horses down to the forest line, taking careful steps on the loose stones and getting there at the same time. Jumping down, he said, 'We better tie the horses up.' His voice broke. Kizzy nodded, her face white and teary.

Jakob wrapped the rope round one of the few pine trees and tried to tie a knot. His hands wouldn't stop shaking. He rested his head against the rough bark, closing his eyes. He whispered, 'Come on, pull yourself together.' Taking a deep breath, he stood up straight and took command.

'You catch Santuzza, Duo and Theo. Check them over for me. I'll see to Herr Engel and Monte.'

His heart felt like a stone in the pit of his stomach as he walked towards the crumpled mass of man and horse. Even from a distance he could see lots of blood and misshapen limbs. It didn't look good. No wonder the eagles were gathering.

Monte moved first. He raised his head. Jakob gasped. A deep gash had opened wide just below his eye. A slab of meat with sinews and oozing blood. Grabbing at his mouth, he tried not to retch.

'It's all right, boy.' Putting his hand out, he stroked his neck. The stallion's skin twitched under his touch. His sides were heaving, every breath an effort. Monte tried to stand, but his foreleg folded underneath him.

'Oh, Monte,' said Jakob.

The horse fell back down with a grunt. The leg was badly twisted.

Herr Engel groaned.

'I'll be back,' Jakob told the horse.

He kneeled by his guardian, who also had a cut on his forehead. Blood trickled down the side of his face. 'Are you all right?'

'Bloody stupid question. I've just slid down the side of a mountain. What do you think? Stupid boy,' said Herr Engel, irascible as ever.

'Sorry,' said Jakob. He wasn't sure what else to say.

Herr Engel tried to sit up, turning to look at the stallion. 'What about Monte?'

Jakob shook his head. 'I think his leg's broken, it's all skew-whiff. He tried to get up but couldn't. There's a wide gash under his eye too.'

His guardian groaned. 'Are you sure? Let me see.'

He tried to stand, but like the stallion his leg gave way. 'Argh!' Collapsing to the floor, he grabbed at his calf. All the colour drained from his face. 'Damn! Monte's not the only one with a broken leg.'

Jakob glanced down. There was a crimson stain spreading across Herr Engel's breeches. He knew he should examine him. Taking off his sweater, he rolled it up. 'Here put this under your head.'

Herr Engel lay back. His face was pale and sweating. He stared at Jakob then across to Monte. The stallion lay on his side, his coat dark with sweat and blood. 'You know what you've got to do, don't you?'

His guardian's meaning sunk in slowly.

'I can't...' Jakob whispered.

'You must. It's the kindest thing to do. There's no one here to help us. Hurry up!' He looked up the mountain. 'See if you can find my saddlebag and bring it here. It must be up there somewhere.'

His head fell back onto Jakob's sweater. His eyes closed.

Jakob stood up and scanned the mountain. In the distance he saw Kizzy leading the stray horses back down. He walked up, collecting all Herr Engel's belongings where they'd fallen in the scree. Most had survived unscathed, including his saddlebag. He headed back with a heavy heart.

By the time he got back, Kizzy was sitting with Herr Engel. She spoke first.

'The others are all right, mainly. They have a few cuts and grazes where they slipped. I looked at Raluca. His knees are grazed as well, where you fell.'

Herr Engel and Jakob glanced at each other and then between Kizzy and Monte.

'What?' asked Kizzy. She looked across at Monte too. 'No! Can't we do anything?' She ran across to the stallion and knelt down, stroking his neck. 'Oh Monte!'

She looked at Jakob. 'Do it quickly.'

He felt sick.

'She's right,' said Herr Engel. 'But first you need to take the other stallions further down. Make sure they are tethered securely and can't see what's going on. They've had enough upset.'

Kizzy and Jakob collected all the stallions together. They were all on edge, prancing around. Raluca called out to Monte. Another lost friend.

They led them down the mountain until they found a perfect place, an area slightly further on, where there were more trees, and where the two children could tether the stallions just out of sight.

'Now be good, back soon.' Jakob rubbed Maestro's flank as they walked away.

'Do you think they know?' asked Kizzy.

He nodded. 'They understand everything.'

When they got back to Herr Engel, he handed Jakob a revolver.

Jakob looked at it, shocked. 'I didn't know you had one of these. I've never used one.'

'It's kinder. You know we can't heal his broken leg, certainly not up here.' He looked round. 'The shotgun would just fill his brain full of pellets. It's ready to go, just point and pull the trigger. Be careful.'

Jakob walked over to the stallion. The horse seemed so helpless. He looked back to his guardian. 'I don't know how to do it.'

'I'll do it then.' Herr Engel tried to stand again.

He let out a mind-shattering scream and fell to the floor, breathless. 'It's no good. You have to. Think how Bauer did it. Aim straight for his forehead.'

The girl let out a sob.

'Come here, Kizzy.' Engel held out his hand towards her.

Jakob closed his eyes. He didn't want to think of Bauer. But choice didn't come into this. He took a deep breath and opened his eyes slowly.

He stood in front of the stallion. He lifted his arm and pointed the gun straight at the horse. This time Monte didn't even try to raise his head. His eyes were rolling. 'I'm sorry, lad.' For the briefest moment the horse seemed to lock eyes with Jakob before closing them. They both knew it was time. His hand trembled. He steadied it with his other hand. Kizzy quietly sobbed; he could hear Herr Engel, with a very weak voice, trying to soothe her. Holding his breath, his finger found the trigger and squeezed it.

The sound of the shot resounded around the valley. Monte twitched then sighed. He'd gone.

Jakob gazed at the dead stallion. His blood had splattered all over the daisies that struggled to grow in the sparse grass. It mingled through the flea-bitten colour of his coat. He couldn't hold it in any longer. Bile from his stomach filled his mouth. He dropped the gun down, vomiting and sobbing as he crumpled to the floor.

He wasn't sure how long he'd been there before he felt Kizzy shaking his shoulder.

'Herr Engel says we need to get a move on.'

'Shouldn't we bury Monte first?' asked Jakob.

His guardian leant up on his elbow. 'No time. Cover him with branches and make sure you take the tack off. Tie it on Theo. I'll ride Maestro. You lead Santuzza.'

Jakob glanced at Kizzy but said nothing.

The two children worked quickly and quietly, lost in their own grief. Soon Monte was covered and all the horses sorted again and ready to go.

'Now let me look at your leg,' said Jakob, worried about the size of the crimson stain. 'It's bleeding. I've got to cut your breeches.'

'If you must,' said Engel grudgingly. He lay back on the floor, still pale and sweaty.

Using his knife, Jakob cut through the material and exposed his lower leg. The cut wasn't as bad as he feared, but the bone was out of alignment.

He checked with Kizzy. She raised her eyebrows. Jakob went blank for a moment, then had an idea.

'Right, Herr Engel, I need to straighten it.' His guardian paled visibly. 'If I pull it straight, Kizzy will tie splints on.' He glanced around for more inspiration. 'We could use branches, couldn't we? That'd be all right?' he asked, doubting himself. The others nodded.

Kizzy jumped up and ran to the trees. She came back moments later with a long, straight piece of birch. 'Get a move on, help me strip and split it.'

They pulled the leaves off and Jakob used his knife to split it in two. He ripped another of his shirts into strips. 'Are you ready?'

Herr Engel nodded. He was positively grey now.

'Here, bite on this.' Kizzy took a shirt strip and tied it into a knot. Engel put it in his mouth.

Jakob took hold of his leg and pulled. He felt the bones shifting. There was a loud crunch as it straightened. Jakob swallowed a mouthful of acid. He knew how tough Engel was, but this was unbelievable. He held the leg taut, so the bones didn't move, while Kizzy fastened the handmade splints to his leg.

'I'm sorry if I hurt you.' She glanced down at Herr Engel as she tied the shirt pieces as tight as she could. He barely nodded, sweat pouring down his face. When she'd finished, Kizzy gave him the last of the water and wiped his face. 'You're amazing.' She kissed him on his forehead.

'Phuff, stuff and nonsense,' said Herr Engel. Kizzy looked hurt for a second, until Jakob saw him take hold of her hand and squeeze it.

His guardian got his breath back, then he and Jakob stared at the map together. 'I think we should aim to get here.' Jakob looked at where he was pointing. It was another clearing by a river.

'It seems relatively easy to get to, not too far,' said Jakob.

Herr Engel nodded. 'Now, you need to help me get up onto Maestro. You *must* ignore my screams. I've got to get on him, otherwise you'll have to shoot me too.' He winked weakly before pulling himself up. The very last bit of colour drained from his face. 'Come on, we need to get going.'

Jakob said nothing as he acted as a crutch for his guardian.

'Bring Maestro up here, Kizzy, please. But leave the others where they are for the moment.'

The girl brought the black stallion to Herr Engel.

'Hold him still. Jakob, go the other side and hold onto the saddle.'

Using the saddle, Engel lugged himself up onto Maestro's back. His broken, splinted leg hung down, useless. 'You two will lead the rest. I can't do it.' He stopped, struggling to catch his breath.

This was the first time in his life that Jakob had heard Herr Engel use the word 'can't'. He turned to Kizzy, wanting reassurance, but she appeared as frightened as he felt. Jakob knew it was up to him to get them to Sankt Martin now. No time to feel sorry for himself.

'Don't worry, Herr Engel. You concentrate on staying on. We'll keep it slow.'

They led him down the mountain to the other horses. Jakob leapt on the back of Raluca and grabbed the four lead reins of his horses. They were all prancing around still, pulling at his arms. He felt exhausted. Staying on would be hard for him too. His guardian followed and Kizzy brought up the rear with her four. It took quite a while for them all to settle down again.

The forest took them away from the mountain,

but it was slow going. Every time Jakob looked back, Herr Engel would attempt to smile. His smile was getting weaker and weaker though. He rolled in the saddle.

'There's got to be a better way for him to travel, surely?' Jakob asked the wind. 'Hurry up, Raluca, we need to get him there as soon as we can or he won't survive.'

It took two hours of riding in silence to get to the agreed spot. Even the birds were quiet.

'We're here!' Jakob led them into the clearing. He let out a sigh of relief. Not only were they tucked right away, but there was an old woodman's hut where they could shelter. It couldn't be better. No one could even stumble across them, he felt sure. The mountains towered behind them. Trees surrounded the clearing, which was quite wide, a few tumbled logs strewn across the stretch of grass. He slipped off Raluca's back, letting the horse walk off to the river to drink with the others. He moved over to Herr Engel.

'Right, let's get you down.' His guardian said nothing as Jakob eased him off Maestro's back.

'You're burning up. Are there any Aspirin in your bag?'

'A few, I think. I managed not to forget those.' His voice was barely a whisper. The pair collapsed onto the floor and his guardian groaned.

Going through the bag, Jakob found the pills. He filled a cup with water from the river. 'Here, take these. They'll help.' Herr Engel was too weak even to hold the cup. Jakob lifted it to his parched lips.

Jakob slowly helped him into the woodman's hut and settled him down. His eyes closed as soon as his head hit the rolled sweater pillow.

Stretching, Jakob walked over to Kizzy. 'He's so ill. I'm not sure he'll last another day's riding. We need to think of something.'

She was busy pummelling herbs for poultices again. She spoke without looking up. 'There's an old Roma way we could try?'

'What's that?'

'We build a sled-like thing from wood. We can pad it with blankets and one horse pulls it.'

This seemed a wild yet sensible plan. Jakob could think of no alternative. 'What do I need to get?'

This time Kizzy stopped and concentrated on him. 'It's a bit like a triangle. You need two very long, straight branches and several medium-length ones. If you get those, I'll get the fire burning so I can boil water for these poultices. I don't want any of those cuts or grazes to get infected.'

Jakob bent down and put his arms around her, giving her a brief hug. She was so thin. Before he could stop himself, he kissed her on her cheek. 'Thank you.' She flushed pink.

Chapter 16

It took Jakob longer than he thought. By the time he'd found and cut down as many straight branches as he could, Kizzy had set the fire and cooked a fish stew and put the poultices on the stallions' cuts. He found her kneeling by Herr Engel, helping him sip the stew.

'Is that enough?' he asked, pointing to the pile he'd made.

She peered past him and nodded. She rested Herr Engel's head back down. He went straight back to sleep with a groan. 'Think we should eat then start. I've redressed Herr Engel's cut, putting a poultice on it first. You're right, he's very weak.'

Jakob stared at his guardian. His skin was like parchment, while his breathing was rapid and shallow. Jakob sighed. 'The faster we get him to Sankt Martin the better. Let's get on and make the sled. Sleep can wait.'

She nodded.

Once they'd eaten, Kizzy picked up a reed and waved it under Jakob's nose. 'Look what I've found. I'm going to make twine with it.'

He swatted it away. 'Gerroff!' He picked up one of the branches. 'Should I strip it?'

Kizzy gazed at him, eyebrows raised. He shrugged his shoulders, trying hard to suppress his irritation. Why couldn't she take anything seriously? 'I was just asking.'

He worked with his knife, stripping all the twigs and leaves off. 'Is this right?' He held it up again. It was as tall as him and as wide as his arm.

Kizzy was too busy constructing an intricate plait of reeds. Jakob noticed that the tip of her tongue was poking out of the corner of her mouth. He smiled, wondering if she knew she did that.

'Ow!' She sucked blood from her thumb. 'Stupid reeds keep cutting me.' She still didn't move.

Jakob tapped his fingers against the branch, trying to squash the ever-growing knot of tension in his stomach. When she finally got to the end, she glanced up and smiled. 'Yes, that's brilliant, but you need another one like that.'

'Thanks – I'd never have guessed!' Jakob's laugh

was hollow. Kizzy gave him a look. They both knew how serious this was.

They worked on in silence.

After several hours, Jakob said, 'I'm done. You?' He walked over to where Kizzy was sitting.

'Yes, me too.' She spread out several long lines of twine. 'Let's lay it out on the floor and then tie it together. See if I can remember how it works.' She rubbed her eyes and yawned. 'I'm so tired.'

'I know, but we're nearly there.' His words were swallowed by a yawn too.

Between them, they tied all the branches together, making the triangular frame just as Kizzy described. When they'd finished, she stood back. She put her bloodied hands on her hips. 'Lift it up and let's see if it is wide enough to fit round a horse.'

Jakob picked up the two long branches. Immediately several of the smaller branches fell to the floor. The twine that Kizzy had spent hours making just wasn't strong or long enough. Her face fell. She threw down the rest. Stomping towards a log, she kicked it, not once but repeatedly, getting harder and harder. Chips of bark flew everywhere.

Jakob dropped the branches and ran to her. The last thing he needed was another injured person. He pulled her round to face him, but she wouldn't look at him. He could see her eyes were glassy with tears.

'Stop, Kizzy, it'll be all right.'

She snapped straight back, eyes hard and dark now, 'No, it won't. Don't you see? I messed up. He'll blame me. We'll never get him there without it.'

She tried to snatch her arms away. Jakob wouldn't let go, gripping tighter, hoping he wasn't bruising her.

Engel groaned in his sleep but didn't wake.

Jakob knew Kizzy was right, but there had to be a way. 'Will you stop it!' He shook her slightly, knowing he sounded harsh. Kizzy looked shocked. Jakob softened his voice. 'Of course Herr Engel won't blame you.' Then he spotted the answer. 'Would it work if we had rope?'

'Course it would, but we haven't any, stupid. Unless you want to go back to Leizmann and buy some. I'm sure those Nazi soldiers would love to see you.' She pulled away and wiped her sleeve across her nose.

'But we do. Look!' Jakob pointed at the leading rein attached to Raluca's halter. 'We have twelve of them, plus extra, I'm sure. We could use the reins to lead them just for tonight, couldn't we?'

Kizzy jumped up and kissed Jakob smack on the mouth. 'You're a genius.' She ran to Raluca, taking off his halter.

Jakob was taken aback. He touched his lips with the tip of his fingers. Had she really just done that? He knew his ears were blazing red.

'Don't just sit there!'

Jakob came to his senses as she began letting the stallions free. 'Kizzy, stop! Don't take everything off. We only want the ropes. We need the bridles on so we can tether them using the reins.'

She stopped and looked at Raluca, who now had no halter or bridle on. The stallion threw his head back, rolled his lips back and blew, whinnying.

'He's laughing at you!'

'Damn!' she said, trying to grab Raluca. No chance. The stallion pranced to one side before standing behind Jakob, resting his muzzle on his shoulder, watching Kizzy.

'Hello, lad,' said Jakob as he slowly put his arm round the stallion's neck. 'Pass me a bridle,' he whispered under his breath.

Kizzy's face was beetroot-coloured and she wasn't in the mood for subtlety now. 'Harrumph, let's get on with it. It's getting late and we don't have much time.' She flung the bridle across to him. Raluca tossed his head into the air, startled by the low-flying tack.

'Careful!' But Jakob was laughing on the inside, even more so when Raluca nudged him. 'That was wicked. You're such a tease!' he muttered under his breath, slipping the bridle back on.

Before long they had collected all the ropes. Jakob wished he'd thought of it earlier; it was much easier making the frame with them, despite his cold hands. Best not to say that to Kizzy though, he decided, after she'd worked so hard on the twine.

When they finished for the second time, the sun was low in the sky and the light was fading rapidly.

'Shall I try it again?' asked Jakob.

'Yes,' said Kizzy, trying to stifle another yawn. 'Keep everything crossed.'

She stood there with her fingers, arms and legs intertwined.

In his head he said his silent prayers again. He knew this had to work. Jakob moved to the front of the frame and picked up both poles. The structure was much stronger. He glanced across at Kizzy and grinned.

'Look.' He shook the frame from side to side. The poles didn't move, and the frame stayed solid. 'You did it, Kizzy.'

Tears of relief trickled down both their faces. 'No, *we* did it,' she said. Neither had slept all day, but they didn't care. Adrenaline kept them both going … just.

'Let's eat, then sort the horses out. I'm not going to wake Herr Engel until we're ready to go,' said Jakob. He found two dented tins of soup and a chunk of stale bread in one of Herr Engel's bags. 'We don't have to hunt this down,' he said, waving them around.

Kizzy laughed and flopped by the fire. 'In that case, you can cook them. I'm so cold and exhausted. It's your job.'

'What's all the noise?' Herr Engel grumbled.

'Oh, you're awake,' said Jakob.

'No bloody choice with all that shouting.' His guardian pulled himself up to a sitting position, wincing. 'What are you cooking?'

'Soup, do you want a bit?'

'Is that all we have left?'

Jakob sighed. 'Yes, 'fraid so.' He poured the soup into three mugs and handed it around.

'It'll have to do. Hope you've been resting. Are you ready for the last bit of the journey?' Herr Engel took the soup and drank.

Kizzy looked at Jakob, who shrugged and said, 'Not quite. We've built you a sled. It's over there.'

'And what do you expect me to do, sit in it?'

'Yes,' said Kizzy. 'You can't ride again, it'll kill you.' She folded her arms and stared Herr Engel down.

'Says who?'

'Says me.' Jakob had decided to take no nonsense. He'd never spoken back to Herr Engel but now he had no choice. 'We need to get to Sankt Martin today and with you riding we won't. We have to move faster.'

Herr Engel said nothing. He went back to his soup.

Jakob lost his appetite. The food tasted of nothing but he knew he mustn't waste it. It was lukewarm, so he glugged it down, before going off to tack up the horses. Maestro was the oldest and most placid stallion, so wouldn't panic at having to pull the sled. Jakob tried to make a bed in it. He rolled up one of his sweaters and put it at the top. He then placed Kizzy's blankets at the bottom to add padding. They could use Herr Engel's own blankets to keep him warm.

'More than ever, we need your Sunday's child luck.' He didn't want to think what would happen if the cantankerous old groom didn't get better.

'You better show me the way, Herr Engel.' Jakob put the map down in front of them.

Herr Engel gave him a strange look. 'I think it's time you called me Heinz, don't you, particularly if you're going to be in charge?' He tried to wink at the boy. Jakob half smiled. His guardian focused on the map. 'It's relatively easy now. Follow the river and then cut through farmland here to get to the *Schloss*.' He pointed.

'I hope you're right.' Kizzy was dampening down the fire. 'I've had enough excitement for a lifetime.'

Heinz grimaced at her.

Jakob laughed. 'Let's tie the sled to Maestro.'

He held onto the contraption as Kizzy reversed the stallion in between the poles. She held him steady while Jakob pushed a branch through each of the leathers above the stirrup irons and tied it as tightly as he could. Moving over to Heinz, he leant down so his guardian could use him as a crutch again. He wrapped his arm around his waist. Jakob was sure he'd lost weight.

Heinz hesitated. 'Are those my ropes keeping that thing together?'

'Yes, we had no choice.'

Edging forward, Heinz's broken leg caught on a tree root. 'Argh!'

Jakob grabbed hold of his guardian as he passed out. He was a dead weight. Kizzy ran forward. Between them they lifted him up. 'That's it, easy does it,' said Jakob as they eased Heinz towards the sled and lowered him into it. The poles pressed down on the leathers as the sled took the weight. Maestro shifted and stumbled, confused by the strange sensation.

'Ssh, lad, it's all right.' Jakob clicked his tongue.

Herr Engel groaned as he came round.

'Are you all right?' asked Kizzy, holding his hand. Her face was almost as pale as his.

He nodded, then in a very weak voice he mumbled, 'I'm sorry.' She squeezed his hand.

'Kizzy, can you hold on to Maestro's reins while I get on Raluca?' She nodded. Jakob pulled himself up on the stallion's back. 'If I take him, Theo and Amato and you ride Pluto, can you lead the rest? I know it's a lot.'

'Of course! I *am* Roma, you know!' She winked, handing him Maestro's and the other horses' reins before leaping onto Pluto's back. 'Let's go.'

'You ready Herr … Heinz?' asked Jakob.

'I'm sure I could ride,' grumbled the groom, seemingly recovered from his faint.

Jakob wasn't going to discuss it. He pulled the reins together. 'Are you ready?' It was time to finish this journey.

Kizzy made a noise.

'I'll take that as a yes.' He squeezed his legs. Raluca looked round at him and nodded. Jakob smiled and shook his head. If he hadn't known better he'd have thought the stallion had just told him it was all going to be all right. The horse moved forward with the three others following behind. Heinz groaned.

'You all right?'

'Yes, just get me to Sankt Martin.'

'Kizzy, how about you?' he shouted over his shoulder.

'Yes, we're just behind you. Don't worry.'

The train of horses and people moved off through the forest. Jakob tried to ensure that he took the smoothest route possible. It wasn't always easy and every now and then he heard his guardian groan. It felt like a spear being thrust through his heart, but what was he to do?

After several hours riding, the landscape began to change. 'We're moving on to farmland,' Jakob shouted to Kizzy, 'so keep your eyes peeled. We're vulnerable now we're out in the open.'

'All right,' Kizzy called back.

It had been so hard trying to avoid the tree roots and it was a relief to get onto more even ground. However, with the moon shining as brightly as it was, it wouldn't be easy to hide ten grey horses, one black one, a broken groom and two children. The moon was rich and buttery. It was time to pray.

Heinz had been quiet for the last hour or so. Jakob tried to look back but couldn't see him.

'Is he all right?' he shouted back to Kizzy.

'Sleeping, I think. Are we nearly there?'

'Not far.'

'Good! I'm exhausted; these beasts are pulling my arms out of their sockets.'

Jakob knew exactly what Kizzy meant. Every bone in his body ached and his head was pounding. He wanted to stop and sleep forever.

They got to the road as the world lightened. Clouds the colour of purple bruises filled the sky. It should be only half a kilometre along the road, but that was plenty long enough to bump into any number of Nazi convoys. The change in surface caused Heinz to stir. He groaned loudly.

'You all right, Heinz?' Nothing. 'Kizzy?'

'I can't see, sorry.'

Jakob took a risk and pushed the stallions into a trot. He waited for the complaints but there was silence. Now he was worried.

'Come on, Raluca, we need to get him to Sankt Martin.'

Up ahead the sun was breaking through the clouds and in the distance he could see a sign.

The baroque *Schloss* wasn't far. It looked like a fairytale castle. Jakob hoped this one had a happy ending.

So nearly there. Please don't let us get caught. Jakob felt vulnerable as they trotted along.

After what seemed like hours, they clattered into a yard near the *Schloss. Please let this be the right place*, Jakob prayed. Lights went on and a man came stumbling out, pulling his braces up over his shoulders.

'What the…?'

'Is the Director of the Spanish Riding School here? We've brought the young stallions and Herr Engel; he's hurt. He's broken his leg.'

The man's hand shot to his mouth, 'Oh my God, Heinz. The Director is inspecting the horses.' He shouted, 'Director, Director! Come quick.'

An elegant man came striding into the yard from the *Schloss*. Jakob vaguely recognised him. It was Director Alois Podhajsky. Were they here? Were they finally safe?

'Heinz? Is that you?' The Director came towards them, his arms wide. 'I thought when you didn't respond to my message that the Nazis had got you.' He clasped his chest. 'I can't believe you're safe.'

Jakob tried to explain. 'Didn't you get our message? We got here as soon as…'

Relief and exhaustion swept over him and he slumped in his saddle. The pounding in his head got worse. Jakob could hear a buzzing noise. He looked round. Where was it coming from? The sound evaporated and a black mist came down over his eyes. He felt himself fall and then a burst of pain in his head. That was the last thing he knew.

Chapter 17

Jakob felt rays of sunlight warm his face, piercing his closed eyes, adding to the pounding in his head. All his limbs felt heavy. He let out a deep sigh. Things felt out of sorts. If the sun was that high in the sky, he must be late for the stables. Why hadn't Herr Engel dragged him out of bed? He hated laziness. What had happened? Jakob couldn't quite remember. He creased his forehead, trying to grasp a memory just out of reach. He groaned and rolled over. The ache in his head swelled.

'About time you woke up.'

Jakob's eyes flew open. That was a girl's voice. He tensed. There was a girl in his bedroom. That couldn't be right.

He tried to sit up. The hammering in his head got worse and a wave of nausea swept over him. In the corner of a bedroom that wasn't his sat a girl on a rickety wooden chair. She was leaning against a chest of drawers at a very dodgy angle and looked likely to fall at any moment. But she didn't seem worried. Her skin was nut brown against her white shirt, and her short hair was shiny and brushed.

'You've gone a funny colour. Are you going to pass out again?'

'I don't know. I feel sick.'

Kizzy rolled off the chair and passed Jakob a bin into which he promptly threw up. He flopped back on the pillow. She dampened a cloth from a bowl on the chest of drawers. Without a word she wiped his face. He hadn't the strength to object. After a bit she spoke, obviously unable to bear the silence.

'You've been asleep for *two* days!'

This seemed a problem. He felt even more confused.

'I know you banged your head really badly and they said you were weak after the journey, but really! This place is huge and I want someone to explore with.'

Slowly the jigsaw in his mind slotted back into place. 'Is Herr Engel all right?' He tried to get up again.

She pushed him back down. 'Stay where you

are. The doctor said you have to until he's seen you. And as for Herr Engel, you're meant to call him Heinz now, remember?'

Jakob tried to shake his head. It hurt. He was surprised he couldn't remember something that important.

'He's not been great but he's doing better. The leg was a bad break, but we did a good job splinting it.' She smiled at him. A memory of the grey-faced groom screaming came back to Jakob.

'The horses?'

'All groomed and well fed. All their cuts are healing, thank goodness. The men won't let me near them though. Because I'm a girl!'

Jakob closed his eyes, sighing, 'We really got here.'

Kizzy chuckled. 'We did!'

There was a knock at the door. Jakob opened one eye.

'He's awake,' shouted Kizzy. He grabbed at his head.

Two men came in. One seemed familiar, but the other Jakob didn't know. He stooped and had thin grey hair. In his hand was a battered leather case.

'Good to see you're awake, lad, if a little pale. You gave us a fright, toppling off your horse and knocking yourself out, you know?' said Director Podhajsky. 'This is Dr Stein. He wants to check you over.' The Director looked across at Kizzy. 'Time for you to leave, young lady.'

She huffed as she walked out of the door. Jakob was relieved she'd gone before the doctor threw the sheet back and peered down at Jakob's body.

He raised an eyebrow. 'Oh, you're circumcised, Jakob?'

Jakob realised quite how bare he was. His face flushed in panic and he covered himself with his hands, pulling his shirt down. He screwed his eyes shut. He couldn't face what would happen next, now they knew he was Jewish.

A cool hand rested on his shoulder and a knot of fear twisted in his stomach. Opening his eyes, he saw the doctor smiling at him. A smile that reached his eyes.

'It's all right, Jakob. Don't worry. No one knows you're a Jew and no one will, not from me. Will they, Director?'

He turned to Podhajsky who shook his head. 'We've looked after you so far. You're a horseman first here, boy. A damn fine one, too, from what they've been telling me. You saved Heinz and my stallions. Nothing else matters. Remember that.'

Jakob blinked back tears.

The Director moved away. 'How long till he's fit enough to help in the yard?'

'Let me just check his head and chest, but I'm certain he'll be well enough soon. Don't you think, Jakob?'

Jakob sat back up, ignoring the pain in his head, and tried to get out of bed. 'Oh, yes, sir.'

The doctor pushed him back down. 'Hold on. Let me do my checks first. You had a nasty head injury.' He took a stethoscope out of his case, put it in his ears then placed it against Jakob's chest. It was cold and made him shiver. 'Breathe in for me, please.'

He attempted to draw in as much air as he could.

Dr Stein took out a small torch and shone it at Jakob's face. 'Follow the light with your eyes.' Finally, he said to the Director, 'Yes, all good. Let him rest again today. Tomorrow he'll be fine to help out. Ease him back into it, though.'

'Can I see Heinz?' asked Jakob.

The Director looked at Dr Stein. 'Yes, it would do Heinz good to see him.'

'Is he all right?'

'He's not as young as you,' said Director Podhajsky. 'And he's badly hurt.'

Dr Stein interrupted, 'But you did a good job with his leg. You and Kizzy probably saved it.'

The Director nodded.

Kizzy came bounding back in. Jakob grabbed the sheet and covered himself up.

'Hang on, young lady. Never heard of knocking?' asked the Director.

Kizzy was breathless and seemed not to care she was being told off. 'Oh, I know, but I was listening outside and I want to take him to Heinz.'

The two older men smiled. 'Kizzy, don't wear him out. I want him fit enough to work with the horses tomorrow.'

'What about me?'

The Director patted her arm and walked out.

She put her hands on her hips and for the first time Jakob realised she was wearing a skirt. A black look flitted across her face. 'Why does he do that?'

Jakob shrugged his shoulders.

'Get up then!'

He blushed crimson. 'I'm not getting dressed while you're still in here.'

'Why not? You did before.'

He laughed, 'That's because there was no choice. I'll dress quickly, I promise.'

When he stood up, the room swam. He felt sick again, but tried to focus on finding his clothes. Determined to see Heinz, he washed and dressed as quickly as possible. The jodhpurs felt good. Someone had put the photo of his parents by the bowl on the chest of drawers. He stopped a moment to look at it.

Kizzy was singing outside. 'Get a move on, will you? You take longer than a girl to get ready,' she shouted.

Jakob opened the door. 'Ssh. I'm here, aren't I? Let's go to Heinz.' He stood, waiting for her, not knowing where to go.

'Ooh, get you, all smart now.' She pushed him round and round then danced off down the corridor.

'Hold on, will you?' Getting dressed had left him exhausted. He felt clammy as he stumbled into a side table covered in porcelain horses and had to stop them tumbling over. The last thing he wanted was trouble.

Kizzy twisted round. 'Oh not again! You've gone that funny colour. Are you all right?' Taking his arm, she pulled it over her shoulder. 'Lean on me. We can do this together.' She half laughed, 'You'd never have lasted as long as me living in the open if our little journey makes you this ill!' Jakob didn't know what to say as the room span once more. She glanced up at him and squeezed his arm. 'It's this way.'

She led him downstairs to another corridor of doors, then stopped and knocked on one of them, opening it without waiting to be asked.

'Look, Heinz, look who I've brought to see you,' announced Kizzy as they tumbled into the room.

Propped up on several pillows was a frail old man. Jakob didn't recognise him immediately. His skin was still parchment-coloured and his eyes sunken, but at the sight of Jakob he smiled. His eyes sparkled silver.

'Good to see you. Are you better? They said you knocked yourself out when you fell.'

Kizzy slipped out, leaving the two together, closing the door carefully after her.

'Apparently I slept for two days. I don't remember it. Are you all right?'

Heinz stared down at the bump in his sheet. 'They've put a cage over my leg. Hurts like hell but it'll get better.'

'Kizzy says the horses are well.'

'Yes. I think the Director is more worried about the mares now.'

'Why? Where are they?' Jakob gazed out of the window. The sun was high in a clear blue sky. Beneath him was a stable yard. He saw a uniformed man leading a stallion across the yard.

'Don't you remember the Führer took all the mares and now the Russians are heading their way?' Heinz tried to ease himself further up on his pillows.

'Yes of course, will the Germans let us get them?'

'No chance. The Russkies will probably eat them before we get there.'

Jakob swung round. 'That's awful. We rescue our horses only to find the others are in just as much trouble?'

'That's war for you.' Heinz closed his eyes. Jakob turned back to watching the horses, lost in despair. Had saving their stallions been a waste of time when the mares were in such danger? Perhaps they could save the others too? Behind him his guardian started to snore softly.

Chapter 18

Two days later, Jakob was in the huge kitchen of the *Schloss*, sitting at the long table, with Kizzy, the Director, his wife, the Countess who owned the *Schloss* and various other people from the Riding School. He'd been trying to learn their names, but he'd never been very good at that. He kept quiet, watching everyone as they had breakfast. Kizzy, on the other hand, was at the centre of the conversation, as always. He smiled while she regaled them once again with the story of how they'd built the sled and saved Heinz's life. It seemed to get more elaborate and dangerous every time she told it.

The smell of warm bread rolls wafted around. Taking a sip of coffee, he glanced across at the Director. Should he ask him if he could ride? He took a bite out of his bread roll, the sweet plum-flavoured *powidl* dribbling down his chin. Jakob scooped up the escaped jam with his tongue, hoping no one had noticed. Two days of taking it easy was long enough for anyone. He'd had enough of mucking out and cleaning tack.

'Jakob, I think you're well enough to ride today. I want you to exercise Raluca and Pluto after you've mucked out the stables. Nothing testing, just a walk round; stretch their legs gently after that long journey.'

'Yes, sir.' He grinned. Out of the corner of his eye, he saw Kizzy sitting up straight, waiting to be told what to do too. Instead the Director pushed his chair back, stood up, drained his coffee cup and went to leave the kitchen.

'What about me?' Kizzy's eyes sparked.

Jakob held his breath as a flicker of annoyance flitted across the Director's face. He stared directly at her. 'Oh yes, you. I forgot about you,' he sighed. 'You can clean the tack. Make sure it's done properly.' He marched out without a backwards glance.

Kizzy looked across at Jakob. 'What's wrong with me?' She threw her arms wide.

Jakob rubbed his face. He knew how tough it was for Kizzy. It couldn't be easy having lived on your own for so long and done everything for yourself to then find people telling you what you can and can't do, but he didn't know how to help her.

'Oh, don't worry, dear. I'm sure he didn't mean it. We can find a little job for you in the house if you'd rather,' said Frau Podhajsky, smiling and patting her arm, missing the point totally.

Kizzy pushed back her chair with a screech and stormed out.

'Ah, I don't think she liked your idea,' the immaculate Countess noted, half smiling as she sipped her coffee. She appeared quite dainty, her dark curly hair peppered with grey. Jakob had heard tales of her escapades throughout the war. The fragile appearance belied the hard woman inside. She didn't suffer fools.

Jakob shook his head. 'I'd better go after her.'

'You're a good friend, Jakob,' the Countess said to his back.

He found Kizzy in the stalls, shovelling muck hard and fast. There was a smell of sweet hay and dung. The stallions shifted in their stalls, nickering a welcome, but for once Jakob paid little attention. He knew he needed to help his friend.

'So it's all right for me to ride the stallions to

bring them here? But now I'm supposed to be some girl who just cleans the tack, if that? It's not fair.' She stabbed the fork into the straw.

Jakob grabbed her arm. 'Stop! Irritating him will not help. The Director's old fashioned. We just have to win him round.' He hesitated, because he knew what he was going to suggest wouldn't do that either but…

He took a deep breath. 'Why don't you come with me when I ride?' What was he saying? He couldn't believe those words had just fallen out of his mouth.

'But the Director didn't say…'

Jakob peered around, hoping no one had heard him. 'He might not have said you could, but he didn't actually say you couldn't, did he?' He grinned at Kizzy, whose eyes lit up. She couldn't see the knot of panic in his stomach. But it had made her happy. He had never felt so torn.

'Come on then, lazy bones. We better get moving.' Kizzy bounced across the stall.

Jakob rolled his eyes. How could she swing from one mood to another so quickly?

An hour or so later they'd finished the mucking out.

'Hello, Raluca.' He patted the stallion's neck before he slipped his bridle on. 'Ready for a walk?' He leant into the horse and rubbed the stallion's neck. 'Stay there while I tack Pluto up for Kizzy.'

But before he could do anything, he saw her riding the stallion bareback out of the stall.

'Do you ever ride with a saddle?' He peered out of the yard, checking the Director wasn't around. That lump of guilt sat heavy on him. He picked Raluca's reins up and led him out into the sunlight.

'No, can't see the point.'

Jakob mounted Raluca. The two children rode out of the yard, heading towards the fields.

Leaning against the gate was a tall, unshaven man with a cigarette hanging from his lips. His hair hung down, limp and greasy. A heavy coat swamped him. He looked up at the noise. There was a spark of recognition in the man's eyes. The refugees who were staying in the grounds of the *Schloss* had warned them about a man hanging round, Wilhelm Faber, a troublemaker. Some said he came from Ukraine, others said Germany. Everyone told Jakob to keep out of his way. From their description this must be him. Fear rippled through Jakob's body.

Faber stared at them as they rode by, puffing at his cigarette. 'Riding bareback, I see. Once a Roma always a Roma.' He smirked, then spat at them. A large globule landed on Pluto's rump.

Kizzy snapped round, her eyes flashing.

'Don't…' Jakob reached across and touched her arm. 'That's exactly what he wants you to do. Don't give him the pleasure.'

She huffed but looked away, moving Pluto into a trot.

'Keep him walking, the Director said,' he shouted, but Kizzy ignored him.

'Yeah, listen to your little Jew friend,' snorted Faber.

Jakob's heart missed a beat. How did he know that?

'Reckon there's money to be made here. She won't be so cocky soon enough,' he shouted, before he stalked off.

Pluto's hooves clattered on the road as Kizzy rode off towards the field. Jakob looked behind, checking no one else was watching.

A gentle breeze blew through his hair and the sun beat down on his back. It felt so good to be on Raluca, who responded to the lightest touch. He sat deep in the saddle. The war and the Nazis could have been a million worlds away.

When the stallions reached the field, they both danced around, skittish in the spring sun. Frothy clouds raced above them. Kizzy and Jakob laughed as the horses lifted their legs high and walked on.

'Let's canter!'

'But the Director said…' Jakob muttered.

Kizzy rolled her eyes. 'Do you do everything you're told?'

'Hold on a minute, I was the one who told you to come and ride with me. That's not fair.' He felt miffed.

Kizzy pushed Pluto forward into canter and then gallop. Pluto's tail looked like silk flowing behind him.

'Kizzy! We're not supposed…'

Raluca snatched at his bit. Pulling hard, the reins ripped into the skin on Jakob's hands.

'Ouch!'

Raluca reared, snorting, throwing him off balance. Jakob grabbed onto chunks of mane.

'All right, let's go!'

It was thrilling. The rhythm of the stallion

galloping beneath him was amazing. 'Go, Raluca!' shouted Jakob. Kizzy turned and waved at him. He'd forgotten how much he enjoyed just riding. Laughing out loud, he chased after her. Dropping the reins, he threw his arms wide, standing up in the irons. 'Kizzy!' he shouted, balancing in the saddle. She turned to see what he was doing. Raluca galloped faster. Jakob couldn't stop grinning. She would not be beaten and did the same.

'I've got an idea. Here, have Pluto.' Kizzy jumped down, thrusting his rope at Jakob. 'Have you got a handkerchief? The Countess keeps giving them to me.'

'What?' Jakob pulled a slightly grubby one out of his pocket and threw it at her.

Kizzy took it between two fingers, wrinkling her nose and holding it at a distance. 'Ew!' She ran off. 'Watch and wait.'

Jakob was intrigued. A few moments later she raced back, having stuck two long sticks into the ground. Each one had a fluttering flag attached to it.

Kizzy leapt back onto Pluto. 'Right, race you to the bottom. On the way you have to grab the flag as you fly by. Yours is on the left.'

'Ha! That's easy. Go on three?'

Kizzy nodded.

'One … two … three!'

Both horses charged off at full gallop. Jakob kept an eye on his flag. He put his reins in one hand and moved down so he was in line with Raluca's neck. 'I can do this,' he whispered to his horse. However, when he got to it, he was too far away and so was Kizzy. They both missed their flags.

'Damn it!'

They pulled the horses up and swung them round.

'Let's do it again,' said Kizzy, trying to regain her breath.

'You're on!'

Kizzy counted this time, 'Ready … steady … GO!'

They flew up the field. Raluca's mane whipped Jakob's hands. He manoeuvred the stallion as close in line to the stick as he dared. Leaning right down, he pushed the horse on. Putting his arm out, this time he grabbed the white cloth with ease. Standing in his stirrups, he yelled, 'Yes, I got it!'

As did Kizzy, shouting at the same time. They were ecstatic.

Both were hot and sweaty, their cheeks flushed pink. Neither saw the Director striding across the field towards them.

'What the hell do you think you're doing?' He grabbed Raluca's bridle. 'I told you to walk them.' He snapped round so he was facing Kizzy. 'And I don't even remember telling you you could ride.'

Jakob looked down. 'I…' The white cloth hung limply in his hand.

'Don't! Take these horses back. They're overheated, so you'd better rub them down as if your life depended on it. Then I'll see you in my study. I can't believe you've been so stupid.' He stared straight at Jakob. 'I'm really disappointed, and with you in particular.' The Director strode back the way he came, shaking his head.

Jakob's head dropped. All the joy of the moment gone.

'I'm so sorry,' said Kizzy. 'I was the one who pushed you. I'll explain, I promise.'

'But I could have said no.'

Jakob was devastated. How could he have been so stupid? The world had just cracked and shattered in front of him. There was no way the Director would ever let him be a Cadet now and all because he tried to make Kizzy happy. So stupid. 'Come on,' he snapped. The frothing clouds now looked bruised to match his mood, and it had grown cold.

The pair rode back to the yard in silence.

Jakob slipped off Raluca's back and pulled his saddle off. The stallion's coat was dark with sweat. 'I'm sorry, boy, I should've thought and I shouldn't have let *a girl* make me do it.' He put a bucket of water down in front of him. The horse drank thirstily while Jakob rubbed him down with straw.

No, that's not fair. I can't blame Kizzy. It was my fault. I just wanted her to be happy. He hugged the stallion and turned to go. 'Are you ready, Kizzy?'

'Yes.' She emerged from Pluto's stall. There was straw in her hair but Jakob didn't remove it. 'Maybe we'd be better off if the Nazis came and took us.'

He stared at her. Jakob's stomach tightened and his heart began to race. 'Don't you EVER say that! Never, ever. Do you hear me?'

Chapter 19

Kizzy's words kept going round and round in his head as they walked from the stables to the *Schloss*. An ugly voice was shouting somewhere. It jarred him and dragged him to the present. The voice was familiar. It couldn't be?

He grabbed Kizzy's arm, pulling her against the wall.

She tried to break away. 'Oi!'

He put his finger to his lip. 'Ssh!'

He shuffled along, flat against the wall. Each crunching step on the gravel echoed around them. Jakob held his breath. When he got to the bushes, he knelt, pulling Kizzy down by his side, and peered through. He gave out a long, deep gasp. He was right.

A large black Mercedes was parked at the front of the *Schloss*. Beside it stood the Director, his arms folded, listening to two Nazis. One was an SS officer, but not any old SS officer.

Bauer!

Jakob gulped.

'He's here!' whispered Kizzy. 'How did he find us?'

'Listen.'

Jakob noticed Bauer had a new scar on his forehead. He wondered if he got that when he fell, dead drunk.

Someone else stepped forward. Jakob grabbed Kizzy's arm. 'Oh God, Faber!'

They heard him say, 'I told you, he's got a Jew boy and a Roma girl here.'

Without missing a beat, the Director said, 'Excuse me, are you accusing my children of being Jewish and Roma? Unforgivable. Take it back at once.'

Faber laughed manically. 'How can they be your children? They're too close in age.'

'They're twins.'

'They don't look identical.' Faber pushed the Director.

The Director held his ground and rolled his eyes. 'One's a boy and one's a girl.' Sarcasm dripped from every word.

Jakob felt sweat trickling down his back.

Bauer poked his gun under the Director's chin. 'Are you taking me for a fool?'

He'd heard those words before and knew how dangerous the man could be. He muttered, 'We've got to do something.'

'What?' said Kizzy.

'I don't know.'

As he desperately tried to think of something, things got far worse. Heinz appeared and hobbled up to the Director, using a broom as a crutch, his face white with pain. Bauer recognised him.

'You! I shot your horse.'

The Director recoiled. 'You did what?'

Faber interrupted, 'They came with him!'

Bauer jumped on this and pointed the pistol at Heinz. 'You said the boy was your nephew.'

The Director immediately responded, before Heinz had a chance. 'Yes, this man is my brother and my children were with him to keep them safe from the bombs in Vienna. Wouldn't you want to protect your children? I sent my daughter down later as she'd been ill.'

'I told you at the time,' said Heinz, leaning hard on his broom.

Jakob was amazed at the number of lies

tripping off the Director and Heinz's tongues, but he was thankful.

'They're lying!' Faber shouted.

'Get the boy here and make him drop his trousers!' suggested the other Nazi, who had thick glasses and piggy eyes.

'What? This is ridiculous,' said the Director. 'I can go and get their papers if you wish?'

Bauer pushed his pistol into the Director's stomach. 'Don't you go anywhere!'

Jakob had a mad idea. He looked at Kizzy. 'Do you fancy going for a ride again?'

'What? Now? Don't be stupid.'

'Hurry up, we've got to be quick.'

He dragged her away, whispering to her all the time. A broad grin stretched across Kizzy's face as she listened.

Near the stables one groom was leading a tacked-up Flavory and another had Largo in a halter. 'I am sorry, but we need these horses. We'll explain later.'

Kizzy leapt onto Largo's back in one easy movement, snatching the lead rein from the groom.

'Hey!'

'Ssh – please, it's a matter of life or death for the Director! Trust me.'

The young man nodded, looking worried.

Jakob scrambled onto Flavory's back, not quite as elegantly as Kizzy. Twisting round, he signalled to her, telling her to go round the other side. 'You realise we only have one chance?'

She nodded. 'I'll hoot like an owl when I'm in place.'

'Go as quietly as possible.'

Jakob kept his horse tightly controlled until they were in place. It felt strange sitting on a different horse, but Flavory responded well. His dark steel grey shone in the sun.

Bauer and Faber were still shouting. He could see Bauer aiming his pistol at the Director, who had been knocked to the floor. Jakob shivered. They were running out of time.

He heard the sound of an owl echoing around the yard. With relief, he gathered his reins, and whistled back. Urging Flavory straight into a gallop, he charged at the gathering of men. Aiming for Bauer, he focused on the pistol.

Jakob heard shouting, but ignored it. The feel of the powerful animal beneath him was extraordinary. Adrenaline pumped through his veins. He moved with the rhythm of the gallop, leaning forward and holding the reins with one fist so he had a free hand. He rode with purpose. Briefly he could see Kizzy charging towards them, too, Largo's grey coat catching his eye.

Bauer stared at Jakob, legs apart, pistol aimed right at him. He was focusing. Jakob pushed Flavory on.

The sound of Kizzy and Largo behind him briefly distracted Bauer. It was only a tenth of a second, but gave Jakob enough time. He reached the officer, stretched down and snatched the gun out of Bauer's hand. The metal felt cold as Flavory flew past the other men, sending them all tumbling out of his way. Kizzy barged in the opposite direction, leaning far, far over, and as the other Nazi fumbled to reach his gun, she whipped it straight out of his holster.

Jakob pulled Flavory to a halt and swung him round to face them all. The Nazis and Faber were straightening back up, having lost their footing in the chaos. The Director got up before going to help Heinz.

Jakob, sitting silently on Flavory, pulled the pistol up and aimed it at Bauer. His finger found the trigger. This would be for Allegra.

Chapter 20

The look of anger on Bauer's face melted into ugly fear.

The Director walked calmly forward. 'Give me the gun, Jakob. You don't want to do it. He's not worth it.'

Tears blurred Jakob's view. 'But he killed Allegra and he was going to kill you and Heinz.' His hand shook.

Reaching up and resting his hand on the gun, the Director pressed gently till Jakob lowered the pistol. 'Yes, he is the scum of the earth, but shooting him will make you no better. Give it to me.' He whispered, 'You are very brave and just saved our lives, I believe. I thank you for that.'

Jakob let go of the pistol with a sigh, letting his head droop, tears streaming down his face, for Allegra, for his parents, for everything that had happened.

Kizzy drew alongside and gently rested her

hand on his. He didn't look at her. He couldn't. He didn't want her to see how much he was crying.

She passed her gun to Heinz, who pointed it at the two Nazis and Faber. The Director raised his gun too. The Countess stood by them.

'Wilhelm Faber, I welcomed you and your friends onto my land and offered you protection when you had no home.' The ice in her voice cut the air. Faber lowered his head. 'You repay my kindness by bringing these people here. I suggest you keep out of my sight.' She moved towards Faber, then whispered loud enough for Jakob to hear, but not the Nazis. 'And if you do anything else to cause trouble I will perhaps tell them,' she nodded towards Bauer, 'exactly who you are.'

Faber nodded and scuttled away, head bowed.

The Director began, 'Bauer…'

He was interrupted by a loud *chit-chat* of bangs. Was someone having a firework display? They all looked up at the skies. Confusingly, there were just clouds. Everyone gasped.

'That's not fireworks, it's gunfire! The Americans must be close.' The Director turned to the Nazis. 'I think you might be a little busy over the next few days. Far too busy to waste time worrying about my children.' He hesitated. 'Perhaps we should lock you up and hand you over when the Americans arrive? Because they will… What do you think?'

The grooms started to move towards Bauer and his associate. The Nazis looked panic-stricken.

'Oh no, you don't. We're out of here. Get in the car quick!' shouted Bauer. They both jumped in. Bauer wound his window down. 'I won't forget this.' He looked at Jakob. 'You, in particular.'

The car sped out of the yard, ignoring the grooms who had to jump out of the way, gravel spraying everywhere. Flavory shied away from the flying stones. Jakob grabbed onto his mane, trying to calm his own pounding heart as well as the stallion.

'Whoa boy, it's OK.'

The Director waved his hand at them. 'I assume you don't want these guns back? That was close! They won't be back. I have every confidence in the Americans. My information is good. I have contacts in the Resistance.' He breathed out noisily though, and grabbed at Flavory's bridle. 'Kizzy, come here. I can't believe you two rode my horses like that after what I just said!' He looked sternly at them both.

Jakob couldn't believe the Director was being so ungrateful!

Kizzy spoke first, 'We just…'

The Director cut straight across her. 'Thank you both for saving our lives. You were brilliant and so brave.' He laughed to see all Kizzy's anger disappear. 'Jakob, can you tell all the men in the School to meet me in the office, then rub these two down and stable them? Do it quickly. Once you have done that you can join us in the office too. Kizzy, I want you to find my wife. Tell her we need all the civilian clothes she saved. Everyone needs to change out of our uniforms in case the Americans think we are the enemy or the military. Heinz, are you all right? I will need your advice.'

Heinz nodded, his face white and drawn with pain. 'Of course.' He turned. 'Thank you two for saving our lives.'

Jakob smiled. 'Director, sir, can I just say I'm sorry I disobeyed you earlier.'

Kizzy looked between him and the Director. 'I'm sorry as well, sir. I'd been badgering him for ages about not being able to ride.'

The Director nodded. 'Let's say no more about it. We've more important things to do now.'

The sky was lightening and the sun stretched long pale fingers up beyond the mountains. It had taken them all afternoon and all night to get ready. The refugees had been assured they would be safe. Exhausted, Jakob walked back to the *Schloss* with the others. Everyone was too tired to speak, but he wasn't ready to sleep. Bauer's last words were an echo in his head. What if he came back? Jakob slipped away to the stables. He knew that seeing Raluca would help him calm down. The stallion whinnied a welcome. Rubbing his neck, Jakob leant against the horse's head.

'Do you fancy a dance, Raluca?' whispered Jakob. 'I've missed it and I need to do something to take my mind off what's happening out there.'

The wind blew gently as Jakob led Raluca to the field. The world smelt clean and fresh. For a brief moment, he felt so happy and safe. Crazy, really.

Letting go of the stallion's halter, he walked alongside him, clicking his tongue. The horse followed him. He watched him.

Jakob stopped.

Raluca did the same, his ears twitching.

Jakob grinned. 'Good lad!' Clicking his tongue, he rubbed Raluca's neck. The stallion whiffled, blowing air out gently. 'So you think you're clever, eh? Try this.'

This time he stood in front of the horse and raised his arms slightly, palms facing outward, walking towards the horse. Raluca flattened his ears, then slowly he stepped backwards, one hoof at a time. 'That's it, well done, boy.' He rubbed the horse's forehead.

Next, Jakob ran forwards with Raluca trotting alongside. He stopped dead. The stallion slid to a halt too.

'Ha!' He threw his arms around the horse's neck, clicking his tongue and scratching at his withers. 'You are a star, aren't you?'

Jakob had an idea. It was an exercise he'd only done once with Allegra, who hadn't been able to do it properly.

'All right boy, watch this!' Jakob stood with his body slightly angled towards the horse then walked slowly, crossing one leg in front of the other. 'Can you do it?'

The stallion snorted and pawed at the ground.

He appeared to watch, before he mimicked Jakob's body language. He arched his neck inwards then carefully crossed his front legs over one another as he walked. Jakob couldn't believe it.

'You're dancing with me!' he squealed. His half-broken voice cracked.

The stallion tried to do everything he did. In his head Jakob heard Strauss' *Vienna Waltz* and visualised the arena with Raluca dancing for him in the centre. A loud rumbling laugh started in his stomach. 'Oh, what a lad!' He flung his arms around the stallion's neck again.

Cheering and clapping startled both horse and boy. Jakob looked to see Kizzy and one of the other grooms, Peter, jumping down from the gate. Where had they appeared from?

'How much did you see?' Jakob asked.

'Most of it,' laughed Peter. 'I bumped into Kizzy…'

She didn't give him a chance to finish. She bounced between the two. 'I saw you sneaking out of the yard.'

'Have you two been practising?' asked Peter, patting Raluca.

'No! That's the first time I've done anything like

that with him,' laughed Jakob, pulling at Raluca's ears. 'He's a natural.' He couldn't stop the pride in his voice.

'No,' said Peter, 'you're the natural.'

There were more echoes of battle, closer now.

'The Americans can't be that far away,' said Peter. The mood changed. 'Take Raluca back. Then check that all the horses have water and hay. I can't imagine the Director will want to put them out to pasture today. He seems confident everything'll be all right, but an army's an army, isn't it, whatever side they're on? Who knows what they might do and if they are going to be friendly.' He started to march off. 'I'll warn him. Kizzy, you run up to the kitchen. They need to get breakfast on the go.'

The *chit-chat* of small gunfire echoed around the mountains.

A thrill of excitement shot through Jakob. He had the same hope the Director did. His parents had been trying to get to America before…

He took Raluca back to the stalls. All the stallions seemed to pick up on the tension in the air. They were whinnying and snorting, pulling at their halters.

'Ssh, it'll be fine, trust me.' Jakob hoped he sounded convincing and didn't over-excite them. He guided Raluca in. 'Hey, let's get you settled. You were a star today.'

He felt the stallion's muscles tense.

'Come on, it'll be all right.'

If Jakob could calm Raluca down, he knew the others would be soothed too. He stroked the stallion's forehead, between his eyes.

The horse's ears flicked to and fro, listening. Slowly his head drooped and he nickered gently.

'That's it boy, it's all right. The world's about to change, but we'll still be the same, won't we?'

Raluca pushed at him with his muzzle.

'I'd better check on the others.'

When he'd finished all the stallions, he went up to his room. It'd been a long night and early morning. The adrenaline rush of the dancing display with Raluca had all but disappeared, leaving the weight of exhaustion and a niggling fear heavy on his shoulders. What if he and the Director were wrong? What if Bauer did come back or if the Americans weren't friendly? He was so confident they were going to be all right but how did he know?

Jakob decided to have a good wash to wake

himself up. Gasping, he splashed himself all over with cold water.

There was a knock on the door.

'Who is it?'

'It's me,' said Kizzy. 'Can I come in?' She opened the door a crack.

Jakob pushed it closed. 'Hold on, just let me get dressed.' He threw on his breeches and a white shirt. It stuck to his still wet skin. 'Come in.'

Kizzy ran to the window. 'Look!'

He craned his neck. 'What am I looking at?'

'Are you blind?' She moved to one side. 'See!'

He peered out of the window. He heard them before he saw them. The unmistakable rumbling, roaring and squeaking of jeeps and tanks moving along the road.

'Are you sure it isn't the Germans?'

She grabbed at his arms. 'Of course not. It's the Americans, stupid!' Pulling him round, she tried to make him dance. 'It's the beginning of the end. Let's celebrate!'

Jakob didn't want to dance. Not yet. What if he had got it wrong? He wanted to share an idea he'd had with her. 'Kizzy, stop a minute. You know the mares?'

She looked at him, her head slightly tilted. 'Yes?'

'Well, we rescued the stallions, so we need to find a way to rescue the mares too.'

'How?'

He looked out of the window. 'I don't know, but I think we should make a pact to try. What do you think?'

'I think you're crazy.' But she bounced up and down.

'Let's shake on it.' Jakob held out his hand. Kizzy shook it, trying to be solemn.

'Come on, let's go to Heinz's room. He'll have a better view than us.'

They bowled into Heinz's bedroom.

'What are you two up to? You both look guilty!' He sat up in bed.

'Nothing!' they said in unison, grinning. They grabbed his arms and pulled at him.

'What the…? Mind the leg… Careful!'

'Look!' said Jakob. He shoved a chair by the window.

Heinz sat on it with a thump. 'What am I supposed to be looking at?'

Kizzy stepped out of the way. 'There, see who's coming…'

Heinz gasped. 'It's the Americans! They are here at last.'

Jakob said, 'But they're going straight by,' as a stream of tanks and lorries passed them. Everyone was cheering and shouting.

'Be patient, young Jakob. They'll be here soon. There's no way they'll miss out a place like this. Kizzy, I want to get downstairs. See if you can find me another broom. My leg's really hurting after all the recent excitement. I think I need two.' She ran off down the stairs. 'Jakob, help me get dressed. I want to meet these saviours in person.' He gripped Jakob's sleeve, his eyes serious. 'You were incredibly brave when Bauer appeared again.'

'No, it was reckless really. It could so easily have gone wrong. We were just lucky.' Jakob let his head drop. 'And I had disobeyed the Director earlier. I let Kizzy ride and galloped the horses when he told me just to walk them. I did what you always told me not to do. I drew attention to myself. If Faber hadn't seen me and Kizzy riding, showing off, he'd never have noticed us. Never have brought the Germans here.'

He pulled Heinz's socks on.

'Yes. Lesson learned, I hope? Ouch!'

'Sorry. Definitely.'

Heinz rested his hand on Jakob's shoulder and squeezed. 'Bet the riding felt good, though?'

Jakob grinned. 'It was incredible.'

By the time Kizzy came back, Heinz was dressed. 'Here we go, I've got a towel to put over the bristles so you don't hurt yourself.' She passed the broom over to Heinz, who smiled.

'Clever idea, thank you.'

She raced ahead and opened doors for them. She bounced all over the place, crashing into every table. 'Are you excited, by any chance?' laughed Jakob, making a grab for a toppling vase.

'Will you be careful, young lady? You need to respect the Countess's property. She's being kind enough to let us stay here. I know you're happy but calm down.' Heinz gave Kizzy one of his looks, but it had no effect.

'Yes, but…' Her words faded into the air.

She ran on to open the door to the courtyard. The sound of their feet crunching on the gravel made the Director turn round. He smiled when he saw them. The smile didn't hide the concern in his eyes. Jakob gripped onto his guardian. He didn't want to be afraid anymore.

The Director said to Jakob, 'I hear you've been working with Raluca?'

Jakob flushed from the base of his neck to the tip of his ears. 'Yes, sir.' Now he was in more trouble. 'Sorry.'

'What's this?' asked Heinz, feigning surprise.

'Peter tells me we have a natural in young Jakob. Needs teaching a little obedience, though.' The Director's stern face fractured into a smile. It stretched right up into his eyes and they glistened with pride. Heinz patted Jakob's arm.

'Yes, yes, you should have seen them.' Kizzy grinned. 'They were dancing. Raluca did everything he did. It's incredible. Director, you must watch him.'

The Director raised his eyebrow. 'Oh, must I?'

Heinz stared at her. 'Kizzy, ssh!'

She stopped, crestfallen, but Jakob smiled, convinced his heart might burst at any moment.

Several jeeps swept into the yard. US soldiers jumped out with guns aimed towards them. Everyone raised their arms in surrender. The Director announced, 'We are friends here. The Nazis are our enemies too.'

One of the soldiers said, 'They're on the run now.'

Jakob noticed how different their uniforms were. They had shorter jackets with myriad pockets, trousers tucked into their boots and funny rounded helmets, all in olive green. A battle-worn officer walked towards the Director and saluted. Not the Nazi salute pointing at the sky. Jakob decided he much preferred this one.

'Sir, we'd like permission to look round.'

The Director stepped to one side. 'The *Schloss* is not mine; it belongs to the Countess.'

The Countess stepped forward. She looked tiny. Jakob noticed her pulling at the buttons on her cardigan. He wondered if she was nervous.

'My apologies, Countess. I'm Lieutenant Colonel Smith and I've been tasked by General Walker with setting up a Brigade HQ, which, with your permission, we'd like to do here. This is a good few miles behind the lines now and safe. It is ideal strategically.' He looked around. 'Plus, it is very beautiful.' The soldier nodded his head in acknowledgement and apology.

'My home is open to you and your men. Please come inside.'

A soldier came running out of the stables, interrupting them. 'Holy mackerel, sir, there's a mass of white horses in here!' he shouted with a twang.

'Really?' Lieutenant Colonel Smith turned to another officer. 'Major Wright, go and see what he's talking about.'

Heinz grabbed at Jakob's arm. 'Check they're all right,' he whispered. 'Be with the stallions, otherwise they might get upset.'

Jakob caught Kizzy's hand. They slipped round the back into the stalls. The stallions were prancing around, unsettled.

'Boys, it'll be all right,' said Jakob. He moved from horse to horse, talking quietly, stroking foreheads and patting their necks. Kizzy did the same, whispering all the time.

Major Wright joined Jakob in Raluca's stall and patted the stallion by his withers. 'Am I mad, or are these Lipizzaners?'

'Yes, they are, sir. The Director evacuated some of them from Vienna, and we brought others across the mountains.'

The officer seemed really comfortable around horses. His eyes were kind as he looked over the stallions. Jakob relaxed.

'You speak English?' Major Wright noticed.

Maybe Heinz's classes weren't such a waste. Jakob smiled. 'Yes, a little, my guardian insisted I learnt English and French. Said it would be useful.'

The Major nodded. 'That's good. I know a little German too.' He hesitated. 'Would your guardian be Director Podhajsky?'

'No, my guardian is a Rider. Heinz Engel.' Jakob was surprised he knew the Director's name.

'Oh, right. I saw your Director win a bronze medal in the 1936 Olympics.' Major Wright pulled at Raluca's ears.

'I didn't know he'd ridden in the Olympics.' Jakob wished he'd listened more to Heinz's stories.

'He was a great horseman.'

'Is,' corrected Jakob.

Kizzy joined the two, saying nothing but watching every move the officer made.

'Point taken, I apologise. My name is Major Wright.'

'I'm Jakob and this is Kizzy.'

He looked round. 'No mares?'

Jakob said, 'No, they're up in Czechoslovakia. We're very anxious about them.'

Kizzy added, 'Yes, we want to save them.'

'Oh, do you? I'd better ask the Director about the mares then, hadn't I?'

Jakob smiled, burying his head in Raluca's mane as Major Wright walked off. He took a deep breath. The stallion smelt of sweet hay. 'Guess what, Raluca? Maybe everything will be all right after all.'

Chapter 21

'Director, this is Major Wright. He recognised the Lipizzaners and asked if I would introduce you.'

The Director was standing in front of his desk, looking grey and lost. Around him numerous American soldiers were moving furniture and setting up office. The senior officer, Lieutenant Colonel Smith, stood over a large map, barking out orders. When Jakob led Wright over and introduced them, the Director appeared grateful for the distraction and offered his hand to the American.

The officer removed his hat and shook the Director's hand vigorously. Wright was younger than Jakob had first thought. His dark hair was cut short and there was a hint of a scar on his neck.

'I'm honoured to meet you, Director Podhajsky. I saw you ride in the Olympics in '36.'

A glimmer of a smile slipped across the Director's face. 'A different time.'

Jakob moved over to the window seat, hoping he wouldn't be noticed and sent away. He looked around for Kizzy, but she was gone.

'Before all this madness.' Major Wright sighed.

'There was madness on its way, even then. You maybe weren't aware.' The Director offered him a chair by the fireplace. Wright took it and the Director sat opposite him.

'You have just the stallions here?' said Wright. 'The girl tells me you're worried about the mares.'

Running his hand through his hair, the Director frowned. 'She shouldn't have said that, but yes, I'm very worried. I confess you've thrown me rather. I'd hoped to build up to this.' He cleared his throat. Jakob listened hard. 'I'd hoped to ask the US army to help me get the mares back. I'm afraid the Russians might destroy them.'

Major Wright leant forward. 'Where are they?'

'I believe they are at Hostau in Czechoslovakia. The Germans took them in 1942. Hitler's aim was to create a perfect breed.'

'Sir, that's tough. I'm not sure what we can do.'

The Director stood up. 'If there's any way you are able to help us…'

Lt Col. Smith came over. 'Is there a problem?'

'No, sir, not at all. We're just talking about the horses,' replied Major Wright.

The officer appeared surprised. 'Oh right, carry on.' He went back to his organising.

Major Wright stood and beckoned to the Director to come close. Jakob strained to hear. 'Look, it's a long shot, but General Patton is stopping at General Walker's headquarters, which is close by. Would you put on a performance? He's a great horseman and a leader of the US Third Army. We could show him how vital it is that we rescue the horses. I can't order something like that. He's one of the few who could.'

The Director balked. 'Goodness, a performance? How long would I have?'

'If I get the message to him today, he might get here in a couple of days. He's a busy man.'

Without thinking, Jakob jumped forward. 'Sir, of course we can do it!'

The Director looked at him. 'Go and get Heinz. I need to talk to him.'

Jakob ran out of the room, straight into Kizzy. 'Come with me. The Director wants to see Heinz. Wright told the Director what we'd said about the mares.'

Kizzy went pale. 'Was he cross?'

'Never mind that.' He didn't wait for an answer, just ran towards the kitchen. 'Heinz, Heinz, the Director wants you.'

His guardian was sitting in the kitchen drinking coffee with the Countess and Frau Podhajsky. His skin still looked paper thin, but at least he had pink cheeks now.

'Slow down, boy. What's the rush?' He turned to the two women. 'So rude! I do apologise.'

Jakob blushed. 'The Director needs to put on a performance. He's worried and he wants to talk to you.' He grabbed Heinz's broom crutch and thrust it at him. 'Sorry, but it's to protect the horses and rescue the mares.'

Frau Podhajsky stood up and moved across to help Heinz.

'It's all right, I'm here.' Kizzy appeared by Heinz's side. She smiled at Jakob. Her eyes sparkled.

Jakob grinned back and pulled Heinz into a standing position. 'Could you help us with the doors?'

'Excuse me, stop rushing. I can manage perfectly well myself, thank you,' said Heinz.

Everyone ignored him and between the three of them they got Heinz to the study. Jakob eased him into a chair, then grabbed Kizzy's hand and led her to the window seat. Hopefully they'd be allowed to stay and listen.

The Director explained the situation.

Heinz stroked his beard. 'Some of the stallions are under-schooled, but it's achievable with the horses we have, and a lot of hard work.'

The Director interrupted him. 'Apart from one major problem. You've broken your leg, and the Nazis took five of the men only a few weeks ago. We don't have enough Riders.'

'How many do you need?' asked Wright.

'To do a quadrille we need eight people, but there's only six of us.'

'Seven,' said Kizzy.

Jakob frowned. What was she up to now?

She walked into the middle of the room. 'You've forgotten Jakob.'

His stomach dropped to the bottom of his boots as the Director laughed. 'You're mad.'

Heinz sat up straight. 'She's not. He can do it.' Jakob blushed. 'He thinks I don't know, but he used to practise exercises on Allegra, the horse that was shot, in the back field. He's good and has a natural, light touch. Plus you heard what he was doing with Raluca this morning and you saw him ride at Bauer. You need to trust him, Director.'

'Sounds like you've an extra man there,' said Wright, crossing his arms and looking satisfied.

'Yes, yes,' shouted Kizzy.

Frau Podhajsky took hold of her arm and made her sit down. 'Let the Director think,' she said quietly but firmly. 'While I go and organise for the uniforms to be retrieved and cleaned.'

Jakob was the only one who'd said nothing.

'Come here, boy. Do you believe you could do it?'

He gulped. 'Yes, on Allegra…'

'Hmm,' grunted the Director.

'Of course you can,' said Kizzy. 'Raluca responds to you like no other horse I've ever seen. You said yourself that Allegra couldn't do what Raluca did this morning.'

Heinz nodded. 'That's true. Why don't you let me work with him, Director, and then I'll let you know?'

Wright said, 'We won't have much time. What is a quadrille?'

The Director explained, 'A quadrille is a precisely choreographed and difficult dance, or it should be...' He looked out into the distance.

'I've got every confidence in you.' Major Wright slapped the Director on the back, who flinched. 'I'll send the message off now, find out when he's due.'

'Sir?' Jakob tried to muster up the courage to speak. 'I remember watching performances and you never did it with an odd number. You said yourself a quadrille needs eight people. We need another rider.' He took a deep breath. 'I think you should see what Kizzy can do too. That'd give us the eight we need. She's a talented rider.'

'He has a point,' said Heinz, tapping his broom crutch on the floor.

Kizzy went very pink.

'But she's a girl!' said the Director.

'She wouldn't look like a girl in uniform; her hair is so short that at a distance no one would know. Let her try out with me. If we're no good then we don't take part,' said Jakob.

'I don't believe this – all right, but Heinz, you better make sure they're good and ready to rehearse tomorrow first thing.' The Director blustered out of the room, shaking his head. 'Unbelievable! Children, not just children, a girl riding for the Spanish Riding School! I've gone mad.'

Heinz turned to Jakob and Kizzy. 'Well, what are you waiting for? Get me out into the yard. We've got work to do.'

Kizzy had a grin wide enough to split her face. 'Thank you for saying that, Jakob.'

'Thank you too. Though you might not be pleased I volunteered you after we've finished. Heinz is a really tough teacher.'

'Yes, I am,' said Heinz, 'now stop talking. Go and change, Kizzy, you can't ride in a dress.' He dropped his crutch. 'Dammit! Jakob, pick it up for me.'

The two hobbled out to the yard where Heinz got Jakob to saddle up Raluca. Kizzy ran into the stalls.

'I think you should tack up Pluto, Kizzy, you've ridden him the most,' said Heinz.

Her face dropped. 'I've never ridden with a saddle or used a bridle with a bit.'

'Well, you're about to learn.'

Chapter 22

'Right, Pluto. Let's get your bridle on.' Jakob slipped the snaffle bit into the stallion's mouth, placing the bridle over his head. 'You all right?' The stallion blew on his hand. It had been a while since he'd worn tack.

Kizzy pushed past, thumping the saddle down on Pluto's back. The horse jerked his head back.

'Be careful!' He rubbed Pluto's neck. 'Ssh, lad, take it easy.'

Jakob watched his friend. Her face was thunderous. 'Ow!' She jumped backwards.

'Now what's the matter?'

'I stabbed my finger doing the girth up. Stupid saddle!' She slapped the leather hard. Pluto jumped again, landing on Jakob's toe this time.

'Ouch!' He pulled his foot out from under the stallion's hoof. 'Poor boy.' He rubbed Pluto's forehead. 'Steady on, it's all right. She's not angry with you.' He turned to Kizzy. 'You can't be like this; it's not fair on him. It's not his fault.'

'I know, I'm sorry, Pluto, it's just this stupid lump of leather. I'm not sure I'll be able to do what Heinz wants.' She looked at Jacob, eyes wide and hopeful.

'Don't worry, you'll be able to do it. Just trust yourself, Kizzy.'

Heinz shouted from outside. 'Hurry up, you two, we haven't got all day.'

An area in a flat field close to the *Schloss* had rapidly been set up as a training arena, thanks to the US soldiers. One soldier brought Heinz a chair, placing it in the centre of the ring. Jakob led Raluca out. Kizzy followed on behind.

'Come on, Kizzy, we can do this.' Jakob gave her a leg up then jumped onto Raluca, who danced around.

'Right, let's warm them up,' said Heinz. 'I want you to move into a trot. Go large, all round the arena. After one circle I want you to travel diagonally, and then across the other way round. Let's stretch those legs and necks in both directions. I made sure it's the same size as the arena in Vienna – fifty-five metres by eighteen exactly.' Heinz stomped his broom crutch on the floor in defiance. Jakob smiled. He knew Heinz would have got it precisely right. He was all about the detail.

Raluca and Jakob led the way. He couldn't always see Kizzy, but he heard her and Pluto. It seemed to go fine. She didn't need to panic after all. He could settle down and concentrate on his performance. This would be a chance to prove that he was good enough to be a Cadet.

'Wonderful, come into the middle.' The two riders pulled up by Heinz. 'Now, Jakob, I want you to go first. Move off, into the trot. I'm sure I don't need to tell you, you always start on the right rein. Go large again.'

Jakob did as he was told. Raluca moved smoothly, responding well to any signals from his legs and hands. He sat deep into the saddle, feeling very secure.

'Concentrate,' he mumbled to himself.

'Good, now move into a canter. I want you to do a flying change.' Raluca performed faultlessly. 'Excellent, how about the *Passage*?'

Jakob wasn't sure he was up to such advanced formations. He asked the horse to move into a collected trot. Raluca lifted his knees in the high exaggerated movement. His neck was strong and arched. They bobbed up and down as they floated along.

'That's wonderful!' Kizzy clapped loudly, startling Raluca, who jumped across the arena. Jakob grabbed onto the stallion's mane, his heart beating madly.

'What did you do that for?' he snapped.

'Stupid,' said Heinz.

Kizzy looked down. Her face was bright red. She appeared to be having trouble staying in the saddle, as Pluto pranced around. Jakob felt sorry for her. *No! Focus on Raluca, not her.*

'Take him down to the walk, Jakob, to calm him down again. When you've done that, I want you to have a go at a *Piaffe*,' said Heinz.

Jakob gulped. He'd only done this a couple of times with Allegra and never particularly well. He replayed the exercise in his head, then asked Raluca to perform.

The stallion arched his neck and lifted his knees high one at a time, just like the *Passage*, but this time staying still. Jakob felt the power rippling through Raluca's muscles. It was exhilarating.

Heinz didn't make him hold it for long. Soon

he asked him to move off from the trot to the canter. Raluca shook his head as Jakob let the reins loosen slightly.

'Let's try a *Pirouette*.'

Holding his breath, Jakob moved Raluca in a circle around his back legs, completing a full *Pirouette*. All the US soldiers and refugees cheered and clapped. Jakob was thrilled and relieved. Raluca had done everything he wanted. He slumped in his saddle, his head falling backwards as he looked to the sky. He'd done it.

'Good, now come down the centre to me. Not bad, lad, not bad. Now, Kizzy, it's your turn,' said Heinz.

Jakob glanced across at her. She looked grey and so uncomfortable, lolling around in the saddle like a sack. He desperately wanted to shout, 'Sit still and deep.'

Pluto danced and pranced around, not paying any attention to her hands or legs. Jakob started to pray. This looked like trouble.

'Walk him round like Jakob did to calm him down,' shouted Heinz, but Pluto just wouldn't settle. Heinz sighed. 'Move him into a trot then, let's see if that works.'

Kizzy kicked Pluto hard. The stallion jumped forward straight into a canter.

'What's she doing?' whispered Jakob, stroking Raluca's neck.

She started to saw at the stallion's mouth, trying to make him turn, pulling at the reins. Pluto's tail swished to and fro and he tossed his head around, fighting the bit. The horse soon gave up and planted all four feet, putting his head down. The abrupt stop sent Kizzy tumbling over his shoulder. 'What the…?' she shouted as she landed on her backside with a thud.

Jakob swallowed a laugh, but the soldiers and others watching weren't so sympathetic. They roared with laughter and pointed. Kizzy's face coloured a deep puce. She stood up, brushing mud and grass off her clothes.

'Enough! Bring him in here, Kizzy. It's no good.'

But she ran off, leaving Pluto standing in the school.

'Get back here NOW!' roared Heinz. Jakob hadn't seen him this angry for quite a while.

Kizzy stopped and walked back to Pluto, snatched his reins up, pulling him towards Heinz. She kept her head down.

'Call yourself a horsewoman?'

'Obviously not. I just fell off, in case you hadn't noticed,' she snapped.

'Stop being spoilt. A true horsewoman wouldn't have run away from her horse.' Heinz rubbed Pluto's neck. 'Never blame the horse for your failings, and never ever take it out on him. If I see you sawing at an animal's mouth like that, you will NEVER, I repeat NEVER, ride one of my stallions again. Now go and untack him. Rub him down properly. He's stressed.'

Kizzy glanced at Jakob. Her eyes were brimming with tears. She wiped her nose before stomping off to the stables.

'You do the same. You and Raluca have done enough for today. Good effort.' Heinz looked sad and grey.

'I'm sorry,' said Jakob.

'Not your fault. I shouldn't have pushed her so hard. I thought she was better than that.'

'She is,' said Jakob. 'It's the saddle and bridle. She's never used tack before.'

'No time to learn, unfortunately.' Heinz heaved himself up onto the broom crutch.

Jakob dismounted and stopped in front of

Heinz. Looking straight at him, he raised his hand in salute. He knew that was the rule.

Heinz smiled and nodded. 'Off you go!' He hobbled off in the opposite direction.

Leading Raluca to his stall, Jakob untacked and rubbed him down. 'You deserve this, you've worked so hard.' He massaged the stallion's leg.

Raluca rested his muzzle on Jakob and blew warm air down his neck.

'Oi, that tickles!'

His laughter stopped when he heard crying coming from Pluto's stall. Kizzy. Jakob sighed. He also heard Pluto clattering around. 'Will you stand still!' she pleaded between sobs.

Jakob peered round the dividing wall. He hesitated, then pushed past Kizzy and stood in front of the stallion. 'Come on lad, calm down, it's all right.' He put his arms around Pluto's strong neck and leant into his chest. Pluto's breathing immediately slowed, matching Jakob's, and the stallion became still.

'Make me look worse, why don't you? How do you know to do that?' growled Kizzy.

'What's the matter with you? Stop taking it out on Pluto. He needs settling.' Jakob stepped back, but Pluto stayed calm and still. He scratched at the stallion's neck and the horse blew gently against his other hand.

'I thought only Roma knew those tricks.'

'Then why didn't you use them?'

Kizzy turned away. 'Because Heinz is right, I'm spoilt and not a horsewoman. I don't deserve to ride after today.' A huge tear etched a path through the dirt on her cheek.

Jakob took her hand. 'That's not true. He shouldn't have pushed you so hard, he said so.'

'I've never seen him so angry. I can't ride on a stupid saddle. I never realised how hard it was.' More tears threatened.

Jakob pulled her into him, hugging her tight. 'Don't worry,' he whispered. 'I've got an idea. Can I just have the old Kizzy back, please?' She nodded into his chest. 'Good! Meet me here at midnight.'

Chapter 23

Jakob crept out of the *Schloss* at ten to twelve. A startlingly bright moon lit his way luckily, otherwise otherwise his plan couldn't have worked. Jakob was taken by surprise when the route was blocked by a soldier on guard.

'Where are you going?' he said, half-pointing his rifle at him.

Raising his arms slightly so the soldier knew he had nothing to hide, Jakob said, 'I am going to teach someone to ride.' He knew how strange it sounded.

'In the middle of the night – are you crazy?'

'Probably, but it's supposed to be a surprise for someone. My friend Kizzy is going to join me soon. Is that all right? We won't cause trouble, I promise.'

The soldier stood to one side. 'Oh go on, but keep the noise down. I can't believe I just said that.'

Jakob went into the stalls, where the stallions were all quiet. He led Raluca out first. 'Wait here while I get Pluto.' The horse stood patiently with his head lowered until Jakob walked out with the other stallion. 'Let's help Kizzy, boys, I know you can do it.'

'Do what?' asked a very sleepy-looking Kizzy.

'Nothing, let's go.'

'It's dark outside.'

Jakob sighed, 'Yes, I know, but the moon is shining, and we've got work to do. Here.' He handed her Pluto's lead rein.

'You've forgotten the saddles.'

'Will you just trust me and get on?'

She shrugged, and took Pluto from him. They both vaulted onto their stallions.

Kizzy growled, 'And?'

'Do you want to ride in the performance or not?' He turned Raluca round.

'Yes! I'm sorry. I didn't mean it. I just can't see how you can help me. I don't even know the names of the stupid exercises.'

Jakob bristled, and through gritted teeth said, 'Well, firstly, they're not stupid, and secondly, I'm going to teach you, if you'll stop moaning.' He softened slightly, and smiled. 'I thought if you learnt to do them without the saddle, we'd then do it with.'

Kizzy looked at him. 'That could work.'

The *Schloss* rose up behind, watching over them. Not a single light was showing in any of the windows. Everyone was asleep, or so Jakob hoped. 'Watch what I do.'

As he performed each exercise, he told her its name. It felt strange at first but Raluca behaved impeccably as always. Jakob's legs hung down loosely and he rolled naturally as the horse walked. Feeling the warmth of the stallion's body against him made him feel part of Raluca as they moved together. It felt good.

'Now your turn.'

Kizzy's face was set hard. 'Here goes. Tell me if I'm doing it wrong.'

'Will do,' he smiled.

'All right!' Kizzy eased Pluto into a collected trot.

'Brilliant, see if you can move into a *Passage*. Use your legs and seat to send the message like I do. Right seat bone, left seat bone, right seat bone...'

Kizzy tried to give Pluto the correct instructions but he refused to move. 'See, I told you he wouldn't do it.'

'Are you really going to give up that easily? Try visualising what you want Pluto to do, use your legs and remember to sit deeply.'

She pushed Pluto on. Suddenly the stallion started the exaggerated movements of the *Passage*. Pluto lifted his knees high, his neck strong and arched.

'He's doing it!' She sounded surprised.

'Of course, he is. He's been trained. Now concentrate and visualise it. I want you to do a flying change. Take him up to canter.'

They worked for another half an hour before Jakob told her to stop.

'All right, now the hard stuff. We're going to put a saddle on and you'll do the same.'

'Do you really think I will be able to do it?'

Jakob smiled. 'Of course I do. Only a moment ago you told me that you couldn't make Pluto do anything…'

Kizzy slipped off Pluto's back and rubbed his neck. Jakob took Raluca to the stable and settled him, before collecting the tack and going back out to saddle Pluto. He gave Kizzy a leg up. 'Right, off you go.'

Kizzy took the reins and moved off.

'Remember to keep your hands light, don't saw at his mouth. Think of the reins as a sponge that you don't want to squeeze too hard, you don't want to lose a drop of the water.'

Kizzy said nothing.

'Go round and do the same things as you did before. The saddle shouldn't make any difference now you know what you're doing.'

Jakob watched with delight as Pluto danced his way round the arena with a smiling Kizzy on his back.

'See! I don't want to say it,' Jakob grinned, 'but I was right, wasn't I?'

Kizzy's face dropped. 'But Heinz won't give me another chance. I was awful and I don't deserve it.'

'Put Pluto away and don't worry. I'll talk to him. He might listen.'

Early the following morning, an exhausted Jakob and Kizzy went to see Heinz. They found him hobbling down the stairs towards the arena.

'Why aren't you with the horses? Are you ready

to rehearse, Jakob? Have you been up all night? You've got black shadows beneath your eyes.' He seemed deliberately not to look at Kizzy.

'I wanted to speak to you first.' He took hold of Kizzy's hand and squeezed it. 'Heinz, please will you give Kizzy another chance today?'

His guardian snorted, 'After yesterday?'

Kizzy stepped forward. 'I know I was very badly behaved. I just wanted it so much. That's no excuse, I know, but Jakob has worked with me all night.'

'I know, I was watching you. He's a better friend than you deserve,' said Heinz. Kizzy nodded. 'Goodness knows why I'm saying this, but saddle up Pluto. This is your last chance.'

The girl squealed, and both children ran forward and hugged Heinz, nearly knocking him to the floor.

'Watch it, will you! I'm a broken man. Go on, get ready. The Director will think I've gone mad.'

They soon joined the others in the arena, riding into the centre. Both looked very proud on their stallions.

The Director stared at Heinz. 'I thought you said she couldn't do it?'

'Just trust me,' said Heinz. He nodded at Frau Podhajsky, who started the music.

Jakob bit his lip, half smiling. This was something he'd dreamt of for so many years. His heart faltered. If only his parents could see him now.

The white stallions performed in unison. Kizzy kept up and did everything Heinz asked of her. Jakob's guardian couldn't keep the grin off his face.

Soldiers came out and watched, along with many of the refugees who had been staying at the *Schloss*. They gasped then clapped as the Director performed a *Capriole*, where his stallion jumped into the air and kicked back with his hind legs.

One day, thought Jakob, one day I'll be able to do that too.

Major Wright marched into the arena. 'Director, I've just received a message. General Patton will be here in forty-eight hours. Will you be ready?'

The Director looked round to all the riders, including Jakob and Kizzy, then Heinz. 'Of course we will. We must.'

Heinz raised his hand. 'In that case, everyone,

let's break for lunch. Go and water your horses and untack them. Director, Jakob will take Africa for you. We'll walk through it this afternoon without them.'

Jakob smiled and leant forward to pat Raluca's neck. He drank in the sweet musky smell. 'Thank you, lad. That was great.'

Chapter 24

Two days and several rehearsals later, they were all dressed in the full uniform of the Spanish Riding School with newly polished tack shining brightly. While they waited for General Walker to bring General Patton over, Jakob walked up and down outside the stables. The sun was high in the sky, hiding every now and then behind scudding clouds. There was a little heat in it, making the sweat trickle down his back. Or was that nerves?

He smoothed down his brown tailcoat, straightening the two lines of brass buttons, smiling to himself. Jakob had never thought this day would come. And here he was, finding it impossible to sit still. His swan-necked spurs clattered on the cobbles as he moved. Waves of nausea swept over him. He hoped gripping hold of his stomach would help.

'You're giving me a headache, Jakob. Will you

stop pacing.' Perched on a stool, Heinz whittled away at a piece of wood with his knife. 'It's no good worrying, you can't change anything now.'

Kizzy walked up to them, pulling at her collar. 'How do you wear these things, they're awful?'

'Gosh!' said Jakob. He'd never seen anyone look so amazing in the Riding School uniform. Heinz dropped his knife.

'What? What have I done?' She checked her buttons then spun round and round trying to see what was wrong. She grabbed at the bicorne hat with its flash of gold braid and pulled it on, the two points facing forward.

Heinz took hold of the hat and gently moved it so it was the right way round. 'Nothing, Kizzy, ignore him,' he said. 'You look fine. Jakob, I suggest you close your mouth or you may end up swallowing a fly.'

Before anyone said any more, they heard the sounds of cars driving up to the *Schloss*.

Heinz moved towards the stalls. 'Right, saddle up and be out front in quarter of an hour. I'll do the Director's horse. It is my duty. Hopefully the leg will behave. If I have problems I will shout.'

Fifteen minutes later, Jakob, Kizzy, Peter and

the other four riders walked out to the arena. The grass had been cut that morning, ready for the performance. Jakob saw Frau Podhajsky standing behind a few flowers, to the side of the arena, with the Countess. They appeared a bit odd, loitering there. At the end of the arena a raised platform had been created and was now full of soldiers who were sitting watching. They had even tried to make it look pretty by putting foliage over the panels at the front of the platform. Jakob wasn't sure it worked. He could see a serious-looking officer sat in the middle. He was covered with numerous medal ribbons on his chest and wearing a helmet. He wondered if that was General Patton. The Director marched over and took his horse, Africa, from Heinz. He mounted, looking very smart as he rode ahead.

The Director shouted, 'Right, let's do a few brief warm-up exercises before we go. See if we can calm these stallions down.'

Major Wright came up and rubbed Raluca's neck. 'Hello, lad. Are you all right?' He looked up at Jakob. 'Let's hope the General understands the importance. Enjoy yourself!' He winked then ran off to the other end of the arena.

'Great, no pressure then,' said Kizzy, who'd gone the same colour as her shirt.

'We'll...' Jakob squeaked, clearing his throat, '... be fine.'

He felt Kizzy's hand slip into his, squeezing it. 'Thank you,' she whispered. Nothing more.

They both focused on the Director and Peter performing long-rein work. Jakob's heart was beating a thousand times faster than normal. This was his dream, to perform as part of a quadrille for the Spanish Riding School. Now it was here, whether he impressed them or not wasn't even the important thing. What mattered was whether they could they save the mares.

Peter was using Burletta, who was a very light dapple grey; a couple more summers and he'd be pure white, Jakob reckoned. Peter walked smartly behind his horse, his boots shining in the sunshine. He held the long reins and a crop in his hand, using only these to guide the stallion. First they trotted up the arena, changing the lead leg as they went. Peter then went diagonally across, ending his section with a *Pirouette* and a bow, then taking the stallion out.

The last to come in before they performed the

quadrille was the Director on Africa. The pure white horse loved to perform. Jakob was mesmerised. Africa did a *Piaffe*, before moving into the *Levade*, taking his front legs off the ground and sitting on his back legs. The crowd clapped. Africa stood back on all four legs and walked off. There was no emotion showing on the Director's face, he just nodded to acknowledge the audience as he trotted past them. Next he moved into the *Pesade*.

'Why's he doing the same?' whispered Kizzy.

'He's not, the angle's different, it is more forty-five degrees, see? Wait and see what happens next.' Jakob had the feeling he was going to end with a *Capriole*. Yes! The stallion leaped into the air and kicked back. The soldiers cheered and threw their helmets and caps in the air.

Jakob sat back, fascinated and full of admiration, determined that one day he would be able to do that too.

'In line, everyone. Start the music. Let's begin the quadrille.' The Director nodded at his wife. Of course, that's why Frau Podhajsky and the Countess were there. The sound of Strauss' *Vienna Waltz* filled the air. Distant memories filled Jakob's head but he knew he needed to focus as they all moved off in unison.

The stallions paraded down the centre of the arena and the performance started. Jakob could feel Raluca tense under him. As he approached one end, Jakob saw Major Wright. He was sitting with the serious man in the round metal hat, who watched the arena intently. He was definitely the all-powerful General Patton. Wright nodded, almost imperceptibly, as they went by. Jakob concentrated on the performance, visualising what he needed Raluca to do.

Everything else, including Kizzy, melted into the background. He listened to the beat of the music and remembered each part of their rehearsals. Raluca seemed to know how important this was too. He held his head high and arched his neck. Jakob felt the power running through the stallion's muscles. This is what they were meant to do.

Kizzy and Jakob were only in the quadrille. When it had finished, they both smiled as they rode out of the arena and stood to one side.

'See, told you we could do it,' Kizzy teased.

Jakob grinned.

As the music finished, two by two they rode up the centre. The stallions walked in unison, stopping in front of General Patton. All riders doffed their bicorne hats and bowed. The General returned the compliment. They lined up in the grass.

The Director moved forward and spoke to General Patton. Jakob couldn't hear what was being said. He and Raluca were standing at the edge of the line-up, too far away. Jakob's heart was in his mouth. The General looked very serious, but other than that no emotion flickered across his face. The Director finished talking and the General merely got up and walked away, Major Wright hurrying beside him.

The Director turned to the riders. 'Everyone dismissed. We've done what we can. It's now in the General's hands. Go and sort your horses out, then the Countess has provided lunch for you all.'

'He seemed quite flat,' said Jakob.

'You're imagining things.' Kizzy let her legs hang out of the stirrups. Undoing the buttons on her jacket, she pulled her collar undone. 'Thank goodness for that, I can breathe again.'

'Get going, you two,' shouted Heinz. 'Get these

horses settled. Once you've eaten, I want you to come back out and polish the tack.'

Jakob let the reins hang loose and leant down into Raluca's neck, breathing in more of his wonderful horse smell from his mane. 'Thank you, you were just perfect.'

Raluca snorted.

'It's going to be all right, isn't it?'

The stallion nickered this time.

'I'll take that as a yes.'

After lunch Jakob found his way back down to the stables. Raluca whickered a welcome. He nudged Jakob gently with his muzzle, snuffling at his hands and pockets.

'What are you looking for? I haven't got anything for you.' Jakob leant his head against Raluca's. It was good to listen to his breathing. The sound of contented horses munching at their feed surrounded him. It calmed him. 'Lunch wasn't much fun, boy, everyone was a bit quiet. Apparently General Patton thought it was strange that we were teaching horses to wiggle their butts, whatever that means. I don't think it is a compliment. I'm just pleased to get away.'

He breathed in deeply. The stables smelt good, saddle soap and linseed oil mixed with Raluca's own distinct smell. So many memories. He closed his eyes briefly as many thoughts slipped into his head, danced around and left. 'Do you think I performed like a Cadet today? Do you think Allegra would be proud of us?'

Raluca snorted.

'We worked so hard to get you all across the mountains, to safety. If we could just do the same for the mares. We can't lose them.'

Raluca lowered his head.

'This General person must save them. Whatever he thinks of us. He just must!' He scratched the horse's neck.

'Oh, must I?' A voice made Jakob jump. He spun round to see General Patton stepping out of the shadows.

Surprised Jakob said, 'You speak German? I speak a little English.'

'I speak some German. But I'm impressed you can speak English. That's what I'd rather we use.' He turned towards the stallion.

'Hello, boy.' The General put his hand out for Raluca to sniff before he moved forward and started to stroke the horse. There was a deep-set dimple in his chin. His mouth was set hard, but his eyes softened when he looked at Raluca. Jakob decided that if Raluca liked him, that must make him a good person.

'I'm sorry, sir, it's just...'

The General spoke across him. 'Let's get some facts straight. I'd rather watch these horses than look at a painting or listen to music. I heard you brought these horses across the mountains?'

'Yes, sir.'

'Why?'

For a moment, Jakob contemplated this question. 'Because the horses needed protecting and I owe Herr Engel and the Director.'

Raluca lifted his head again and nudged the General, who smiled fleetingly at the touch. 'They are certainly beautiful animals. What do you mean you owe them?' He stared at Jakob. 'Can I trust you? Why aren't you fighting for the Germans?'

The question took Jakob aback. It felt like he was being interrogated.

'I'm too young to fight, sir, and anyway they wouldn't let me.' He hesitated. Should he say this?

Did Americans have a problem with Jews too? He took a gulp of air.

The General glanced at him, seemingly aware that there was more to this story. He raised an eyebrow and tilted his head, encouraging Jakob to continue.

'I'm unclean. I'm a Jew.'

General Patton looked confused. 'What the… What do you mean? Where are your parents?'

'I believe they were taken in 1938. We assume they went to one of the labour camps we've heard about, but I've no idea if they're dead or alive. The Nazis round Jews up like cattle. The Director and Herr Engel hid me in the Spanish Riding School to keep me safe, then when it became too dangerous in Vienna, the Director sent Herr Engel with me and some of the stallions, out to a farm.'

Jakob turned to Raluca, praying that the tears gathering in the corner of his eyes wouldn't fall. 'It was all right until a new SS officer arrived. He wanted to see my papers. He shot one of the horses, my Allegra. We couldn't risk staying.'

Jakob sniffed and wiped his eyes, grateful when he saw the General look away.

'And the girl? Is she your sister?'

'Kizzy? No, she joined us when we were travelling. She's Roma, so unclean too. The SS killed her parents while she watched. She was hiding up a tree. Bauer, the SS officer who killed the horse, came here the other day. He was after us again.' Jakob half smiled. 'Hopefully we're safe now you've arrived.'

General Patton looked serious.

Jakob pushed at the straw on the stable floor with his boot. 'Sir, the mares in Hostau, they've done nothing wrong. Who knows what might happen to them. Everyone deserves to feel safe and free.'

The General stopped stroking Raluca's neck and looked straight at Jakob. He cleared his throat. 'Jakob, isn't it?'

'Yes.'

'You're the first person to talk sense to me and to explain why I should help. You've shown me why the horses really matter, not just for dancing. See, you love horses as much as I do, don't you?'

'Yes, sir.' Jakob was not sure exactly what he meant. The American twang made it difficult for him to understand but he concentrated hard.

'I think you've just convinced this old General

to go and save those horses. What did you say again? Everyone…'

'Everyone deserves to be free and feel safe, even horses.'

General Patton nodded and marched out of the stall.

Jakob stood staring at the retreating General's back. 'Raluca, did I just save the mares?'

The horse snorted and pushed at him.

'All right, all right, I know,' Jakob laughed. 'We saved them together, didn't we? We all saved them, saved them all!'

Note: This story is a piece of fiction. However, the US army did rescue Lipizzaner horses from Hostau in a mission called Operation Cowboy. This is an interpretation. An idea. A thought. It is how people who love horses and care about people might just have behaved in a time of fear and desperation before that operation happened.

Acknowledgements

Writing acknowledgements are so hard, there is always a fear you are going to miss someone because writing a book is never a solitary thing, so if I have, please forgive me. First, I'd like to thank Imogen Cooper for being a great friend but also for giving me the courage and head space to write *Flight*. Imogen was also *Flight*'s first editor, challenging me always to make it better. I trust her with my life and my stories. Thanks, Imi!

Secondly, many years ago Andrew Melrose told me my place was in writing for children. He was right. Thank you, Andy! Like Andy, Judy Waite and Judith Heneghan have been hugely influential and fantastic friends, providing amazing support and encouragement throughout all these years. I couldn't have done without you. In fact, I wouldn't be here without the University of Winchester who introduced me to writing for children. I thank them and, of course, all my colleagues, who are a constant source of inspiration and support.

Thank you to the Golden Egg Academy (GEA), the inspiration of Imogen Cooper. Through it I've met and worked with some amazing people. I want to thank everyone there; Abi, who is a star; all the editors and the Eggs, particularly my own who I love dearly. A special thank you to Kathryn Kettle Macdonald and Karen Taylor. You both know why. GEA is a fabulous organisation for aspiring writers. *Flight* would not be here if it wasn't for them and Imogen.

Extra special thanks must go to: Vashti Hardy, James Nicol and Jennifer Killick for answering numerous daft questions and being a constant support; Sue Eves, a star for taking some amazing photographs and being at the end of twitter whenever needed; Jen Morgan, for being crazy; my rock, Debbie Welham, who's permanently on the end of a text message – there are no words for how much she does; Sally Ballet and Chris, who after thirty plus years of friendship, deserve medals.

Thanks also go to Imogen's Rafi, Patrick Kempe and Tetūa, Barry Cunningham, Mel Newman, Barbara Loester, Nikki Puckey, Leonie

Lipton, Stephanie Spencer, Nancy Rosoff, Jen Webb, Tony Eaton, Melvin Burgess, Tim Bowler, Lucy Coats, Cathy Cassidy, Meg Rosoff, Alex Campbell, Sophia Bennett, Tanya Landman, MG Leonard, Rowena House, Eddie Hardaker, Eve Fradgley, my specialist nurse Carolyn Best, and so many people who offered advice and support in many different ways throughout. Writing can be a lonely occupation. It is wonderful to be surrounded by such incredible people.

Flight wouldn't be published if it wasn't for the faith and belief of Penny Thomas and Janet Thomas. They make working with Firefly Press so easy and positive. I'm so grateful to be with such a dynamic and forward-thinking publisher that really cares.

I've been part of SCBWI for over ten years. It's a great group that always supports and inspires. It's wonderful to share this with my fabulous SCBWI Critique group: Nicky Schmidt, Kathryn Evans, Jeannie Waudby, Pat Walsh, Jackie Marchant, Ellen Renner. Also Carmel Waldron, who sadly passed away earlier this year, far too soon. Candy Gourlay was also a member of the group when I first joined so I count her as an honorary member! They've seen me through some tough times.

Finally, I must thank my huge family. Thank you for willingly answering my random questions. I'm so grateful that you all have such eclectic and useful jobs! I wish my parents were alive to see this book being published but am thankful that they always encouraged us to be whoever we wanted to be. The biggest thanks must go to my children, who have stuck by me through thick and thin. It's not always been easy for us, but they've always been there and believed in me. Lastly, a mention for the little people in our lives, they make me smile every day: Noah and Zachary, as well as Bridget and Seb. Love you x